RAVEN'S GLEN

EVERNIGHT PUBLISHING ®

www.evernightpublishing.com

RAVEN'S GLEN

DEDICATION

To Barry—my husband and best friend for almost thirty years. To the adventures we've had and will continue to have.

Also, thank you to Ryan Spring of Choctaw Nation of Oklahoma for kindly (and patiently) answering questions about his beautiful people.

RAVEN'S GLEN

RAVEN'S GLEN

Nancy E. Polin

Copyright © 2020

January 1996

Skylar dreamed of a raven. Huge, it stood on her windowsill, black feathers glistening in the moonlight. Tilting its head, it cast one knowing eye on her before it began speaking. The words didn't sound like they came from the rough confines of a bird's throat. His voice sounded polished and smooth, like river stone. Entranced, she listened and stared, but couldn't quite grasp his meaning. As far as she was concerned, his words didn't make sense. When he finished, he hopped and turned to fly away.

"Please, don't go. I don't understand." She reached toward him, hesitating. Some small part of her was afraid to make physical contact, thinking he might disappear into vapor.

The raven twisted its head. "Be strong, child." He flew into the night, a shadow against the moon, then nothing.

Strong hands clutched her good arm, rocking her back and forth, insistent.

Sky cracked her eyes open, her blurred vision settling on the general shape of her brother. Backlit, she wouldn't have been able to make out his features even if she could focus. At the moment, she couldn't care less one way or another. For a short moment, she wondered if he'd just slipped into her dream again, deciding against it the next. He would have had a bigger role.

"Wake up, Sky!"

Whatever her father had given her made her feel slow, lethargic, and heavy. Blinking, she tried to clear her sight. "Go away, Stephen. I'm tired."

"Get up, now!" His voice cracked and Skylar normally would have laughed and teased him. At twelve, he was six, almost seven years her senior and entering the painful awkwardness between child and man. Any other time she would have been delighted to point it out, but the night had been ... bad ... and now she was too sleepy and full of brain fuzz to bother.

The warmth of her blankets was yanked clear, allowing cool air to settle against her and mingle with the chill from earlier. Stephen pulled her to a sitting position, jostling her shoulder.

A cry popped out before she could muffle it.

"I'm sorry, Sky, I'm sorry." Although not above a whisper, the tone of his voice sounded sincere, but there was something else there, something she didn't want to identify.

He stepped away for a moment and she watched, puzzled, as he pawed through her dresser. Pulling out several articles of clothing, he returned to the bed and shoved them at her. "Hurry. You need to get dressed."

"Wha ... why?"

"Trust me. It'll be okay. You just need to do what I say."

"Fat chance." Her words slurred and she frowned.

In the low light, her eyes had begun to adjust. Blinking again, hard, she narrowed her gaze to focus on her brother. He stared back from an unusually pale face, his expression tense, fearful. That's what was in his voice: fear. Nothing could have scared her more. Stephen didn't show fear. Anger, yeah, disgust, yeah, but fear was something he kept close to his chest. Even on their father's bad days.

"Where are we going?"

"Away."

"What about Mama?"

He hesitated, an icy cloud passing through his brown eyes. "She's gonna catch up. Now stop asking stupid questions and get dressed. Don't forget to put on your long johns. It's cold."

"I wanna go back to sleep."

"You can't yet. You can sleep later. Look, Mama made me promise to take care of you, and I'm gonna do it. Now, get your butt up and dressed. We don't have much time."

"I feel weird."

"I know. You'll feel better soon. How 'bout you just pull your jeans and sweatshirt over your pajamas? You're less likely to trip and fall on your face."

Confused, Skylar did as he asked. For a few moments, she thought she might fall over, but she sat on the edge of the bed and worked her jeans up her legs and over her hips, not liking the feel of her jammie bottoms wadding up underneath. She said nothing though, not wanting Stephen to get even more frustrated with her.

Standing up, she swayed, but Stephen caught her by her good arm. He guided her back into a sitting position before crouching to shove her sneakers onto her feet and tie them. "Okay, Sky, we need to be quiet once we're outside. I've packed a bag so we're ready to go."

"Where are we going?"

"To Mawmaw."

Tears stung her eyes and nose. "But I don't *know* Mawmaw!"

"*Shh!* It doesn't matter. It'll be okay. Do you trust me?" He peered up at her, old eyes settling into a young face.

"No."

"C'mon, Sky."

She pouted, but didn't let her tears fall. "Okay."

"Why are you *still* here?" Their mother's slight figure appeared in the door, clutching her robe around her. "Stephen, what did I tell you?"

Her words held the teeth of panic. "You *need* to catch the 10:45."

"Sky's still drunk, but we're going now." Tears thickened his voice as he stood, throwing off Skylar's thin veneer of control.

"Mama? Why can't you come?" She began sobbing, and Stephen put an arm around her. The gesture made her sob harder.

The woman rushed forward and pressed a kiss to each of them. "I'm sorry, my beautiful girl. It'll be fine. You need to go with your brother. He'll look out for you."

Stephen helped Skylar into her coat before shrugging into his own. He leaned down to grab the large duffle bag and pulled the strap over his head to cross his thin chest.

Their mother walked them out of the bedroom, up the hall, and to the front door. She hesitated again, pulling them toward her in a firm hug. "I love you."

"I love you too, Mama," Skylar whimpered, so tired and confused. She just wanted to go back to bed. She didn't understand any of this.

Opening the door, their mother waved them forward.

Stephen took her hand, an uncommon occurrence, and pulled her forward down the front path, while Mama disappeared back inside.

Sky thought she was crying and that made her own eyes fill.

"It's not far. We'll be there before you know it."

"Where are we going?" Voice shaking, she rubbed her eyes with her fist.

"Bus stop."

She stopped and stared up at him, tears stinging and blurring her eyes. "I don't want to. I want mama."

"C'mon, Sky!" He tried to pull her again, even as she fought him. In exasperation, he let go and she fell onto her butt. Biting his lip, he looked down at her, up and past, and then down again. "We have to go, Sky, now!"

"I don't wanna!" Her wail cut the night and he hissed at her.

"You gotta!"

"I'm tired and I feel funny."

Sighing, he squatted and touched her shoulder. "I know you do, but we still need to go. How about a piggy back?"

Running her sleeve across her nose, she blinked up, doubt swirling within. Steve rarely offered the coveted piggy back. "Really?"

"Yeah, yeah." He straightened for a moment, swung the duffle bag off, and crouched down. "Hurry."

"My arm hurts."

"I know it does. Just do the best you can."

"Okay." She climbed up, awkwardly grabbing around his shoulders with one hand. He caught her legs and heaved her up a little higher, grunting with effort, his bag dangling from one arm. A moment later, he plodded on, eyes forward.

When they were a block and a half away, the biting wind shifted.

That's when they caught the acrid stench of smoke.

Chapter One

Twenty-four years later

As Jack Langham walked into his daughter's elementary school, two main thoughts rotated in his mind. The first was that his daughter had a wicked right hook. That was kind of his fault since he tended to let her take out her eight-year-old aggressions on his weight bag. Second was the fact that too many people were creeps. If the boy hadn't been a creep, his daughter wouldn't have seen fit to punch him. It was a pretty black and white as far as he was concerned.

Of course, the principal disagreed. She'd called to give him the whole scoop on what happened, stopping short of tut tutting. She'd acknowledged the boy's cruelty but still couldn't condone Avery making him cry. At least, not officially.

Just by reading between the lines, Jack suspected the kid had a reputation for being a bit of a bully.

He could smell paper, paint, and the aroma of lunchtime. Just across the hallway, kids sounded like they were cheering on a gladiator performance in the cafeteria.

Jack pushed through the outer entrance of the principal's office, receiving a once, then twice over from the admin. She stared at him from behind thick lenses, trying on a smile that looked like she had a toothache. "Dr. Langham?"

"Yes."

"Principal Dailey is expecting you. Last office on the left."

He nodded, followed her direction and peeked inside the room. The principal sat behind her massive desk, her long, freckled hands folded in front of her. She was anywhere between sixty and a hundred and two, with sagging jowls, laugh lines, and a firm forehead. It was a confusing mix. Across from her, a sallow couple in their upper thirties sat staring at him, their offspring, presumably, between them.

Avery huddled on a chair to the principal's right, head down. She peeked up at him without moving her head.

Jack pulled a chair from the sallow people's row, placed it next to Avery, and sat down. He looped an arm around her and she huddled closer to him. "So, from what I've heard, my daughter drew a picture of her family, which included her deceased mother. Your kid took it away from her, wouldn't give it back, said something really cruel—apparently Ms. Carlisle heard it, so there's no denying it—and now your son is upset and crying because Avery fought back. Do I have this correct?"

Mrs. Sallow opened her mouth and closed it, opened it. Mr. Sallow narrowed his eyes, his lip lifting in a sneer. "Violence can never be tolerated. Your daughter had no right to hit my son."

"So, your kid telling my kid that her mother 'must have killed herself when she first saw Avery's face,' is something that *can* be tolerated? And by the way, her mother was killed in an automobile accident, just for the record."

Mrs. Sallow quickly looked at Mr. Sallow.

Jack presumed this was news to her.

Principal Dailey cleared her throat. "There's fault on both sides. Andrew needs to work on being kind, and Avery needs to mind her temper."

Jack couldn't really argue with that, even if he wanted to.

"Words cannot physically harm, but hitting can.

That child needs to be disciplined." Mr. Sallow continued to sputter, while his wife looked at Andrew, who studied one dirty thumbnail.

"Actually, words can cause intense damage. It's just not as easily seen with the naked eye," Jack retorted.

"I assure you all that both children will be disciplined." The principal raised her voice in a tone that had both kids cringing. "They will both write letters of apologies, will be seated on opposite sides of the classroom from one another, and for now…" She looked at Jack, her face firm, but he thought he saw a hint of compassion in her light brown eyes. "I think you should take Avery home for the rest of today and tomorrow. Andrew will spend the same amount of time doing classroom work in my office."

So, his daughter was getting the boot for a couple of days and the other kid got to keep the principal company. The Sallow people seemed to gloat, but, as far as Jack was concerned, their kid got the worse deal.

He stood up, not bothering to look at the other parents. "Thank you for your time, Principal Dailey. I'm sure this won't happen again."

****

They stepped out into the bright sunlight, but Avery didn't seem to notice. She kept her head down, staring at her sneakers.

"You okay, honey?"

She shrugged.

They reached his truck and he gave her a lift into the backseat, watching while she scrambled into her booster and reached for the belt. "Do you think I'm angry with you?"

"Maybe a little."

"Disappointed, maybe, but to be perfectly honest, that kid's a jerk and his parents are apologists. I will never, ever be angry with you for defending yourself." Intent and truthful, he met her eyes, raising his brows for emphasis.

She stared at him, her dark eyes filling. "You know why I drew that picture of you, me and Mommy with wings?"

Jack shook his head.

"Because I was trying to remember her without looking at a picture."

A pain lanced through his chest and he sucked in a slow breath. It had been almost two years since Nicole died and although he tried to engage Avery with stories of the three of them, her memories were fading. "I see."

"I feel so bad, but then again, I know she's not ever coming back. I just don't want to forget her."

"I won't let that happen, baby, but you're right, she isn't coming back." Jack lowered his voice. He missed Nikki so much, but the ache had finally started to ease a bit. These depressive episodes with Avery had lessened significantly. She'd even tried to set him up with the cashier at the UPS store last week, much to his horror and the woman's amusement. It was a sure sign she was moving on and prodding him to do the same. "We're doing okay though. Little by little. Right?"

She nodded and he shut her door, before climbing into the driver's seat. He started the engine, slapping on the a/c. Turning around, he gazed at her solemn face for a few moments. "Want to go to Sonic?"

A smile twitched at her mouth before fully forming. "Okay."

"You're not going to try to set me up with one of those roller skating servers, are you?"

She seemed to contemplate this for a long moment. "Maybe."

"*Wonderful.*"

Avery giggled and Jack was happy to hear it.

Chapter Two

Skylar Donaghue sat cross-legged in the grass, hands resting on her knees. Heat and humidity rose up around her in blurring waves, while strong rays of sun made her skin prickle. She hid her eyes behind dark sunglasses, gazing at the stone before her.

Two names were etched on the smooth surface: *Phillip Ashbrook and Elizabeth Ashbrook.*

Her grandfather had passed away several years before her birth, but her grandmother's date of death was a mere five months ago. Sky still had times when she'd forget and reality would steal her breath for several long moments. Her eyes would tear and her heart would feel like it was splitting in her chest.

She found it helped to stop by the cemetery and sit within its peace and stillness. Sometimes she'd talk to her like Mawmaw was listening with her usual patient ear, only commenting when necessary. Other times, Sky would remain quiet, listening to the breeze and losing herself in memories.

Her grandmother had been proud of her, she knew. She'd been encouraged every moment, every step, to pursue her education and everything surrounding it.

"You just didn't quite see me graduate," Sky murmured. "But I think you would understand my choice now. Stephen doesn't and I don't think he ever will."

A tear slid from behind her dark glasses. She let it be. It hung at her jawline for a moment, before landing on the back of her hand. Reaching out, she touched her grandmother's name. The stone was uncomfortably warm, but she traced the letters with two fingers. "I love you, Mawmaw and I think I'll always feel you with me, but it's time for me to go."

In one fluid movement, Sky got to her feet and left the cemetery.

****

She wedged her small SUV between a 70's behemoth and a late model import. She didn't expect she'd be long and the ache in her chest throbbed. Persistent by nature, she knew she'd have to give it one more go. After that, well, she'd just have to deal. He'd come around. Hopefully.

The bell above the door dinged when she stepped out of the heat into the air-conditioned front office. Two desks stood separated from the small waiting room by a tall counter, clean with the exception of a house plant, a plastic caddy of business cards, and a display of automobile air fresheners.

A large man with long dark hair pulled back in a tight ponytail sat behind the first desk keying something into the computer. He stopped and looked up at her, a broad smile cutting across his wide face. "Hey, lil sis. When you goin' out with me?"

"One week from never." She shoved her sunglasses on the top of her head while the man guffawed. "Where's Steve?"

"Bay 4."

"Thanks." She headed toward the interconnecting door, stopping at the man's quiet words. Good humor honed from a childhood friendship dissipated from his tone. "He's really upset, Skylar."

Dropping her gaze to the toes of her shoes, she hesitated. Benny had been Steve's best friend since before Sky's memory kicked in and she'd been 'lil sis' just as long. He rarely called her by her given name.

"I know, Ben." Without looking at him, she pushed through the door, the familiar aroma of oil and tires settling into her sinuses.

One of the other mechanics gave her a nod over the whir of an impact wrench before returning his attention to his task. She nodded back without slowing.

Sky approached the last bay, watching her brother's movements as he fiddled around under the hood of an old Jeep. As if sensing her, he spoke without looking up. "You heading out now?"

"Shortly."

He didn't respond, but his actions turned jerky, angry.

Her own anger rose with his and she took a breath to calm herself. They'd already had too many words. "I guess I'd hoped we could at least be on cordial terms before I leave."

Dark eyes appeared around the edge of the hood. "I think I'm too pissed off to be 'cordial,' Sky."

"You realize you're not being fair, right?" She bunched her fists, dimly aware of her nails biting into her palms. She sounded childish to her own ears and it pissed her off even more. "This is a great opportunity for me and you know it."

"All I know is you're deserting your family and your home. You belong here, not elsewhere and definitely not back there. Of all the fucking places you could have chosen!"

Sky spoke through her clenched jaw. "I've worked my ass off and this university position is everything I want right now. As far as going *there* goes, it wasn't like I went out of my way. The job came up in my feed and I just went for it."

"Are you sure?" Stephen stepped from behind the Jeep and crossed his arms over his chest. "I think you've been wanting to poke your nose down there for years now."

He stood before her, a solid man of average height with short ebony hair and penetrating eyes. As always, she was reminded why she'd felt so out of place as a child. Stephen had inherited their mother's skin tone and hair, while she favored the father she didn't remember and no one spoke of.

Sky lifted her chin. "As usual, you're making assumptions. It's a coincidence. That's all it is. The town means nothing to me, and I don't recall one damned thing about it. You *know* that."

"Coincidence. Sure." He shook his head, dropped his arms, and stepped back toward the SUV. "I've got work to do."

"That's it then?" Her voice rose and she struggled to bring it back down. "You've told me nothing about that damned place, and yet I'm supposed to just take your word for it to stay away. It's *just* a town, Steve, nothing more, nothing less."

Her brother had already turned his attention to his job and didn't respond.

"I guess this was a mistake." Pivoting, she walked away, only to hear his deep voice follow her.

"Text when you get there." He said nothing more.

Shaking in anger and frustration, she let herself from the garage back into the office, willing her eyes not to burn. At the very least she'd say goodbye to Benny.

He leaned against the inside of the counter, brows pulled together as he regarded her. "He's worried about you."

"I know." Sky pinched the bridge of her nose and shook her head. "I just wish he'd scale back. We haven't been children for a very long time."

"Old habits and that."

"I guess." She folded her arms atop the counter and tilted her head to gaze up into his face. "Do you

21

think I'm being selfish?"

Benny pulled in a deep breath and held it, before letting it out in a rush, giving her the scent of sour coffee. "Honestly?"

She cocked her head and raised an eyebrow.

"Yeah. Sure. Okay. Um, well, from a tribal perspective at least, you have a lot to offer. You've come a long way from that little kid that followed Steve and me everywhere." He allowed a tiny smile. "I still have a hard time wrapping my head around Dr. Donaghue, you know?"

"In fairness, so do I."

"Even if you're not a real doctor."

"Ha."

"Anyway, teaching your own people would be huge."

"Benny—"

"No, let me finish. Please." He waved one big hand, fingers splayed.

She closed her mouth, biting off her instinctive defensiveness.

"Anyway, what I was going to say is that sometimes we have to cut our teeth out there, ya know? I mean, going to school is one thing, but working off the rez? I tend to think it's a bit different. Not speaking from experience here. Never had the balls. Besides, I like it here. But I've known lots of folks who have gone and stayed away, and a lot more who have gone and come back."

He was right. Family was huge in the Choctaw community. Many would prefer to live in poverty than leave their loved ones. Of course, if he was trying to make her feel better, he was missing the mark. Sky's spirit drooped.

"I'm not trying to make you feel bad, lil' sis. I

think my point got lost somewhere in there. What I'm saying is you have a lot to offer the outside world too and then, God willing, you can bring what you've learned back here. I think taking that job can only lead to good things."

"Thank you, Benny." She frowned for a moment, considering. "What do you think about Steve's superstition?"

The big man sighed. "That I'm not sure about. I don't doubt some places can be bad, but I don't know if that place is really bad or if Steve's just confusing a horrible event, whatever it was—I mean, he never told me and I never asked—with geography."

"Really? He never told you?" Maybe she shouldn't have been surprised, but on some level, she expected Stephen would have unloaded on his best friend. She wasn't even sure if their grandmother had known the whole story.

"Nope. Of course, even if he did, I wouldn't break his confidence. I figure there's a good reason you don't remember and it should be left alone." He straightened when the bell on the door tinkled, allowing two customers in from the heat. Benny nodded to them, holding up one finger. "Anyway, forget about that. Just know we're all real proud of you and want you to succeed. I guess that's the bottom line."

"Thank you." Her chest loosened just a little. "I better head out, but can I ask a favor?"

"You know you can."

"Just watch out for him, okay? You know how he gets."

"You bet. You be safe, lil' sis."

Sky offered him the best smile she could and turned to leave. Tears bit at her eyes, but she refused to let them take over. She had a five-hour drive before her and rampant emotions would only be a distraction.

****

Stephen watched through the bay door window as his little sister climbed into her SUV. She paused a moment, flipped her braid back over her shoulder, and peered back toward the building. Her eyes were hidden behind sunglasses, but she pressed her lips together, hard.

He knew from experience she was just trying not to cry and felt like an asshole because of it.

From the moment she'd been born he'd tried to protect her from herself and others. He'd failed many times, but it didn't stop him from trying. She seemed to think he didn't realize how hard it had been for her up here, at least in the very beginning. The kid stood out from the other children with her fair hair and complexion. As a result, she'd been the butt of teasing and jokes.

She'd also always been on the receiving end of a certain degree of awe. After all, she was the only granddaughter of Elizabeth Ashbrook, a highly respected member of the tribe. Sky emulated Elizabeth, in personality, if not in looks and most folks recognized it. Even as a little kid, she'd stood up to those bigger than her to defend those smaller. It also meant she tended to do whatever the hell she wanted.

His gut burned and he rubbed his stomach, making a distracted mental note to go back to the clinic. His ulcer was acting up again.

"You think acting like an asshole is the way to go?"

"I'm always an asshole, Ben."

The man huffed and stood next to him, gazing out the window to where Sky's vehicle was parked just a moment earlier. "Fair point. I just don't get alienating her. I'm not sure what you're expecting."

"I … ah, hell, I don't even know. At one time she'd listen to me."

"When was that, man?"

"Yeah, yeah. Fine. At least she'd pretend to listen to me, but this going back to Texas thing. I just have a bad feeling about it." Stephen went to pull his cigarettes from his breast pocket. Then he remembered where he was and stopped. "I know it sounds kind of stupid, but I can't help it."

Outside, a large raven dropped onto the thin strip of grass in front of the parking space and hopped around. It appeared to look their way before taking flight. Stephen shuddered, annoyed by his reaction. It was just an animal.

"Well, all you can do is be there if she needs you. Keep being her big brother, man. And don't pay attention to that damned bird."

The words sounded great, and he knew they was sincere, but Steve couldn't help but notice Ben's voice shake just a little.

Chapter Three

When Molly Achen parked her RV on the street just to the left of her driveway, she breathed out a huge sigh of relief. It seemed to start deep in her toes, a pleasant vibration following it all the way up and out.

Yep, God it was good to be home.

For the last few years, she'd spend six months of the year in Wisconsin with her daughter and her family. She loved them to pieces, but condescension once subtle bloomed a bit too quickly of late. Molly wasn't losing her marbles. She was only sixty-nine for God's sake, yet her daughter sometimes behaved as if she were perching on the edge of that slippery slope.

Mom, are you sure you bought those insoles?

Damn straight she did. It wasn't her fault the box boy didn't put them into the bag. A quick call to the local Woodman's grocery proved Molly right. So there!

She'd stuck her tongue out at Denise for doubting her. Her daughter hadn't noticed, but Molly's six-year-old grandson, Max, had and his giggles had been worth the slight.

In fairness, it wasn't unprecedented. Her husband of forty-six years, Frank, had withered away for close to eight years before succumbing to the struggle. At the end, he'd worn diapers and had thought Molly was his mother.

It had almost killed her, but she'd pulled herself up, remembered the amazing man he'd been, and moved on. Of course, when she'd purchased her Class B Winnebago about three months later, it had started some ripples through her daughter's brain. Molly could practically read the, "Oh no, here we go again!" in Denise's eyes.

Silly really. Lots of people her age hit the road. It's not like she was ever even alone while she was on the open highway. Her travelling companion, Mr. Chuckles, not only kept her company, but kept her safe. He was as content with the long bouts of silence as he was with her listening to The Who, Blue Oyster Cult, or Prince. He was the only man she'd ever known who didn't complain.

Yep, Mr. Chuckles was the perfect travelling companion. No one needed to know that the hundred and twenty pound Rottweiler mix was a big weenie.

"Well, Chuck. Finally!"

The dog sat in the co-pilot seat with his belt securely fastened. He looked at her and pricked his ears, smiling in a happy pant.

Molly's mind ticked off everything that needed to be done as she climbed out and walked around to get her dog. First thing, she needed to call AAA to jump-start the Subaru in the garage, after which she needed to get to HEB to restock her pantry and fridge. The house would need to be aired out, but she'd open the windows and light some incense. It would smell like her home again in short order.

She released Mr. Chuckles from his seatbelt and he jumped down and stood by her knee, waiting while she locked the big van up. Molly pivoted to go up her walkway, stopping when she caught a glimpse of the home just east of hers.

The place looked lived in once more. Wind chimes hung to the left of the door and a child's scooter had been left leaning against the few steps leading up to the porch.

"Huh. I guess we got ourselves some new neighbors." Molly stared at the house, her mouth tightening a little. Despite the cheerful façade of the cottage-like home, people didn't often stay long. It had been purchased cheap after that long-ago incident, fixed up on a strict budget, and rented out. In the time since, folks had gone through it, most not staying beyond their first lease. She'd never been particularly surprised by this. Some marks never went away, at least in her experience. Before she'd headed for Madison this past spring, there'd been some contractors working on it, shortly after, the 'for sale' sign appeared.

Molly made an instant decision to bake her famous chocolate chip banana bread and bring it on over to her neighbors. It was the right thing to do. Besides, she'd be lying to herself if she didn't admit she was a little curious. The last time she was over was when she'd shared some tea with old Ms. Bevin. That was before the woman's kids had conspired to stick her in an assisted living place, which was a fancy way of saying she was one step from death, as far as Molly was concerned.

A deep shudder sank in and knocked her bones together.

At the same moment, Mr. Chuckles leaned in against her with a low whine.

Still gazing at the bungalow next door, Molly rested a calming hand on the dog's head, wondering absently if realtors were legally bound to provide full disclosure or if that was just in certain states.

Chapter Four

Sky made the drive in just over four and a half hours, stopping only once for a cherry kolache and to stretch her legs in West. She took the off ramp, traversing the frontage for a short time, before turning under the freeway and pulling into the parking lot of the local extended stay. She hadn't had time to find a place to live and figured she'd work that out as she became accustomed to the area.

She had an appointment to meet with the director of the program and planned to freshen up before finding her way to the university. It wasn't a huge town, so she suspected if she just headed due west, she'd run into it. Preferring paper maps, Sky liked to find her way without GPS if she could get away with it. Stephen always teased her about that little quirk in her personality until they'd been on a road trip between Durant and St. Louis and had lost cell service. Sky had spent the next three and a half months rubbing his nose in it. She'd been fifteen at the time.

Stopping before the glass doors leading into the motel's lobby, she took a quick breath.

No, she couldn't let his attitude bother her. He'd get over it.

Frigid air blasted her when she pushed through the glass door.

The lobby was clean and spartan in a color pallet of cream and burgundy. To her right, a rack pressing against the wall touted brochures for local tourist attractions. Schlitterbahn, Snake Farm, and Wonder World Cave and Adventure Park caught her eye, as well as places in Houston and Dallas. She figured there weren't enough to fill the pockets otherwise. The room spread out to her left with chairs, tables, and a bar boasting toasters, a waffle iron, coffee makers, warmers, and enough space to spread out a fairly decent breakfast for the hotel's patrons.

A tall, skinny man in his early twenties stood up from behind the counter directly in front of her and smiled to reveal a front chipped tooth. The smile broadened a little as his large grey eyes swept over her and he cleared his throat. "Good afternoon. How can I help you?"

His name tag announced him as "Tyler" and Sky nodded. "I should have a reservation under Donaghue?"

He pecked at his computer, squinting at the results, pecking and squinting some more. "Um, yeah. I've got you here for the next two weeks…?"

"Yes, possibly longer, but I'll let you know." She dug in her purse for her driver's license and credit card.

"Relocating? Are you a student?" The tone of his questions held a little more curiosity than she cared for. His gaze found hers and tried to hold it.

She didn't let him but flashed a quick smile to cover up any slight. "Yes, probably, and no." She thanked him when he handed over the key and gave her directions to her room.

****

Going by memory from her previous visit, she left the interstate and sifted her way through surface streets, getting turned around only once before finding her way to the school. A stone sign announced the University and its founding date, aging it just over a hundred and ten years. She guided her vehicle beyond, making a right into the first parking lot.

Once inside, she hesitated. Summer term had just ended and fall didn't start for a couple of weeks, so, with any luck, security wouldn't be ticket happy just yet. Sky passed the front spaces and chose to park closer to the greenery that spread south from the lot. A trail wove through trees, passing benches here and there while circumnavigating a large pond. She thought she could hear the gentle flow of a small waterfall somewhere beyond her line of sight. The school offered environmental studies, and she guessed this natural area allowed hands-on experience. Either way, she found it tranquil, inviting, and worth investigating at a later date.

When she pushed the car door open, any semblance of cool air from the air conditioning was lost in the sultry heat of August in Texas. It wove around her and squeezed, bringing a thin coat of sweat to her brow and relief that she'd dressed in a silk tank top, light cotton slacks, and wedges. She wore her thick hair in a French braid hanging down between her shoulder blades. Normally, she would have opted for something a little more professional, but since this visit wasn't official, she figured she could get away with a more casual look.

The first building towered above the parking lot, standing in contrast to others built in an age of function over statement. Spires and oblong windows set against limestone gave it a classic appearance and Sky liked it on sight. There was something peaceful and stately about it, even though she had no doubt Stephen would find it creepy. He didn't care much for old architecture.

She shook her head and tossed her purse over her shoulder, heading for the broad cement stairs leading to the main hall. Heavy double doors, imbedded with thick glass stained to simulate blue bonnets, invited her inside. The slightly musty scent of an aging building mixed with paper and cleaning solvents filled her sinuses and Sky took a deep breath. It was a familiar aroma, one she associated with academia.

With new excitement, she walked toward the

wide polished staircase, sliding her hand lightly against the smooth, curved balustrade, almost colliding with a tall, dark-haired man coming down.

"Oh, I'm sorry." He apologized, accent more west coast and less Texas.

The man stood backlit against the stained-glass windows at the first landing, so she couldn't clearly see his face, but his voice was smooth and pleasant.

"No worries. I wasn't really paying attention, to be honest. My mind is a little scattered at the moment."

He tilted his head to the side, as if sizing her up, his face still in shadow. It irritated her that he had the advantage. "Know where you're going?"

"I was there only once —a couple months ago— but I believe so. Dr. Elise Brown's office?"

The man nodded. "You're on the right path. Hang a left at the top of the stairs—second floor—and her office is almost to the end on the left-hand side."

"Thank you."

"Any time." He sidestepped her and jogged down the stairs as she continued up.

****

Heart thumping faster than he would have liked, Jack hesitated and turned to catch another glimpse of the woman.

She continued on, likely lost in her own thoughts, but he had enough time to slide his gaze over her, noting the dark blonde hair braided and hanging almost to the middle of her back, the slender waist flaring to slim but rounded hips, and a cute butt. He felt a little like a creep but told himself he was a young physically healthy heterosexual male—it was perfectly normal to look, as long as he didn't leer. That's when it ventured into freak territory.

But, God, those eyes! He'd never seen that particular shade of blue before, enhanced by their almond shape in a face with sculpted cheekbones, full lips, and a small, straight nose. Unable to help himself, he climbed back up the first few steps, craning his neck and hoping to catch another glimpse.

Too late.

Chapter Five

Stephen Donaghue slumped in the corner of his couch, smoking his second from last cigarette of the day. His legs stretched out across the teak-top coffee table right next to his dark phone. A worn photo album, the binding starting to unravel at the top corner, rested across his lap. "My Family" was embossed in silver calligraphy across the front cover.

Purposely avoiding two small boxes in the corner of his living room that had belonged to Mawmaw, he'd spent two hours going through cartons in the garage until he'd come across the album. He just hadn't opened it yet. Stephen expected it would be filled with happy, but deceptive smiles. To be honest, he didn't really remember. His grandmother had had a few surviving boxes shipped up after that night. He'd poked through them, but it had been years ago.

He knew he'd soon get a visitor. Chloe would let herself in the back door and sit beside him before curving her body against his in companionable silence. They'd listen to music (she might exchange the current selection of Kane Brown for Luke Combs or Carrie Underwood), maybe dance a little, or watch a movie before finding their way to the bedroom.

This had been going on for almost two years. He probably loved her, but they'd never talked about it.

His gaze wandered to the far corner where those boxes of Mawmaw's still waited. She'd always kept her home orderly, never one to hold onto anything extraneous. Those two boxes were unmarked and had been stacked just inside her closet. Five months later, he still hadn't opened them, a little fearful he'd tap into the Pandora's Box of his past. Sky had ignored them too, probably for similar reasons.

Leaning forward, he stubbed his cigarette out in the ceramic ash tray Sky had made for him in middle school. It held the shape of a lung, mottled and dark. It wasn't very subtle of her, but he'd shrugged at the time and had used it ever since. It served to remind him of how fleeting everything was. It didn't matter if he smoked or not.

Pulling in a deep breath, he ran light fingers over the front of the album before opening it. The photos were protected within plastic sleeves, but there were empty lines next to each, inviting the collector to write about each one. A shiver crept along his skin when he recognized his mother's writing.

Next to a photo of a dark-haired child on a rider fire engine was written, "*Stevie's first birthday.*"

The writing was frilly, loopy, and young looking. He knew his mother had been only nineteen when he'd been born. His father, John Patrick Donaghue, had been close to thirty.

There were many more pictures documenting his early childhood: "*Stevie's first day at kindergarten,*" "*Stephen at swim lessons,*" "*Stephen at the kids' park,*" "*Stephen and John Patrick fishing*". In most of them, he didn't smile. There was a photo of the three of them standing on the beach. His father grinned, his eyes that peculiar blue-violet, the sun bouncing off his blond, wavy hair. His mother's smile seemed forced and even at her young age, her eyes were weary. She was also noticeably pregnant. Stephen didn't smile in that photo either. At six and a half years old, there was a set to his jaw reminiscent of someone ten years older.

Stephen wondered if he'd ever really been a child.

He looked closer, studying his father's face. The

man had been handsome, charismatic, and could charm anyone. At least, anyone he didn't know. He saved his cruel, sadistic side for home. Sometimes there was a catalyst, whether it was a bad day at work or a crap commute. Other times, he was unpredictable, especially when he'd crawl into his bottle.

The next photo was at the hospital the day Sky was born. He'd been sitting in the armchair next to his mother's bed, holding his sister. She'd been so tiny, barely six pounds. It was one of the few where he wore a smile, even if it was a subtle upturn at the corner of his mouth. He remembered being so proud, but also feeling this breathless weight of responsibility. *"Big brother Stephen with baby Skylar."*

That sense of duty should have eased a little when they'd gone to live with their grandmother. After all, Mawmaw had been one of the strongest people Steve had ever known, and she'd raised her grandchildren with a firm, yet respectful hand. She'd never been one of those adults who claimed absolute knowledge and wisdom over children simply by virtue of age. She listened, discussed, and they all learned together.

But somehow, it hadn't. The responsibility still weighed heavy, even when Sky pushed back, as she often did growing up. Of course, she had every right to be upset with him now. His baby sister was freakin' thirty. It still boggled his mind.

Stephen heard the screech of hinges when the back door opened. He tossed the photo album on the coffee table with a thunk and shifted to watch Chloe sashay in.

At twenty-nine, Chloe Folsom had a strong, lovely face with long, straight, shiny dark hair and sported a figure curvy enough to spark her own dry self-deprivation. Stephen always dismissed her occasional battle with confidence. He loved her extra ten or eleven pounds. They were distributed in all the *right* places.

She leaned over him for a kiss and he smiled onto her soft lips. Her subtle musk, coupled with the scent of window cleaner reached him. Chloe would have just gotten off work at the Kwik Chek where she served as cashier, stock girl, and gas station attendant. Tomorrow, she'd be sequestering herself online for school. She was almost done with her medical transcriptionist training and enjoyed pointing out that she'd soon be able to work from home and someone else would have to sell the Icees and clean the damned beverage machines.

"Hey, babe."

"Hey."

Chloe sat beside him, tucking her legs under her and curling into him. Her head nestled between his shoulder and jaw. She remained quiet for several long moments, but an unusual tension in her body told him she had something on her mind.

"Benny came by tonight."

Stephen sighed, saying nothing.

"He's worried about you." She tilted her head, as if to study his profile. "*Have* you contacted Skylar? It's been what? Two weeks?"

"Not quite. She sent a couple of texts saying she was okay." He bristled, knowing he shouldn't, wishing he wasn't such a stubborn ass. At first, the silence had been in fearful anger. Now it bordered on pride, although his fear hadn't dissipated.

"Not the same. Have you considered how much you might be hurting her?" Her dark gaze stayed glued to his face. "Is that what you want?"

"You sure know how to cut to the point."

"Indeed I do. And?"

He leaned forward to grab his pack of cigarettes

and tapped the last one out. "*Benny* doesn't need to worry about me. And this situation with my sister is complicated."

"I think he's concerned you're going to forever screw up your relationship with Sky because you're a stubborn ass."

He stared at her and frowned. There wasn't a single person on the reservation who didn't have their opinions about what happened the night the Donaghue children came home. As far as he knew, Mawmaw had never confirmed, nor denied, any gossip which had wafted her way. Most folks had heard stories how Nita Ashbrook ran away with the charming, blond outsider, but those stories varied depending on which tribe member one spoke with.

Hell, Stephen barely knew the early roots of his own existence.

"I know." His acknowledgement came out in a whisper and Chloe rested a gentle hand on his leg. "It kills me that she went back there. I just have a really bad feeling. It's not a good place for either one of us."

His voice shook and Chloe narrowed her eyes, frowning.

At that moment, he expected he wouldn't be able to dodge her questions any longer. Maybe she'd even be able to help him dismiss some of his "memories" in favor of a sharp imagination.

He doubted it though.

Chapter Six

"How much of that bad feeling is superstition, Steve? I don't know what happened to your family all those years ago, but logically, she's just in a town like millions of others. And, to be honest, she has every right to be there. Horrible things happen everywhere and people move beyond them. We're tenacious that way." A tiny smile twitched her lips for a bare second before disappearing. "But the bottom line is Sky's a big girl who was offered a great opportunity. And seriously, it's not like she can't take care of herself. Do you remember that whole thing when she and I were in middle school? The infamous Sonny Harkins incident...?"

Stephen smiled despite himself. He remembered and more than a little pride stirred. His little sister had learned to stand up for herself early and from her own experience, she'd instinctively stood up for anyone else perceived as weak or an outsider. Chloe had been a grade behind Skylar, terribly shy and a little chubby.

Sonny Harkins had been a mean little shit and Sky had witnessed him stealing Chloe's dessert and calling her a hog, among other things. She'd stomped up to him, grabbed the brownie, and handed it back to Chloe. The kid took a swing at Sky, who evaded it and retaliated with a right hook that landed square against Sonny's ear. The kid howled and the incident was over. She'd gotten three days in-school suspension, while he'd been booted out for a week. Yeah, Chloe wasn't wrong. Sky could stand up for herself. Stephen had taught her to fight. She'd taught herself the right time and place.

"Besides," she said, patting his leg, "I have no doubt Sky will tell you if she needs you. Well, at least as long as you don't continue being an ass."

"She's just as stubborn."

"Yeah, maybe, but she doesn't have anything to apologize for." Chloe gazed at his profile. "She's your only family now. Don't screw it up."

"Okay, maybe some of it *is* superstition, but to be honest, there's more to it than what happened that night." It popped out before he'd really considered what he was going to say or how he was going to say it, but she looked at him, eyebrows raised in expectation. He pulled in a full breath and released it in slow trickle. "Things … incidents … happened before then."

"Abuse." Her eyes went soft with compassion.

"Well, yeah, there's no point in denying we dealt with John Patrick's shit, but there was something else and it's … I guess kind of hard to talk about without sounding either nuts or paranoid…"

"I doubt you'd even sound either way. Besides, who am *I* to judge?" Chloe gazed at him, meeting his eyes. "Remember, I'm Miko's granddaughter. I'm a joke by default."

He shook his head and sighed.

Her granddad had mockingly been dubbed the Choctaw word for "chief" since claiming some kind of lineage way back to Pushmataha. The man had often been inebriated and showed a great talent for stories, but most folks didn't take him seriously. When he died, Chloe's mother found him in his back shed on April Fool's Day. No one believed the news at first. It was a real shame. Stephen had always liked the old guy.

"We're not always the result of our lineage. If we were, I'd be in deep shit." He kissed her temple. "Besides, your grandfather was harmless. Amusing, but harmless."

Chloe continued to gaze at him, unwilling to be distracted and Steve sighed again.

"All right, fine. Just remember, I did warn you."

"Duly noted."

Stephen paused for a long moment before nodding. "I liked to build and fix things when I was a kid. Not unlike now, I guess. When I could get away with it, I'd use the old man's workbench. Next to it, he had this big storage unit and I was looking through it for another box of nails and came across these … *books* hiding behind some crap on the bottom shelf."

"Books. What kind of books?"

He shook his head, his breath whooshing in his ears. "In retrospect, occult, but all I remember is the artwork being horrific. I was probably twelve or close to it, and I'm looking at pictures of severed limbs and heads, screaming people, while other were laughing. There were drawings of people having sex, some being raped. I wanted to burn the book, but I couldn't help but be a little fascinated. I'm not sure what that says about me."

"You were a kid. Kids are intrigued by awful things."

"Yeah, well. Anyway, John Patrick caught me and grabbed my arm. It was unusual—most of the time I was too fast for him. He said it was none of my business, but he also said something along the lines … to be honest, I'm not sure if I remember correctly because he was kicking the crap out of me at the time … but I thought he said that he was inevitable."

"Inevitable?" Chloe blinked moisture from her eyes. She'd often get teary about his past. "What does that even *mean*?"

"I'm not sure. All I know is when I healed, I rode my bike to the library and researched the one book. It dealt with cults through the ages, up to and including modern ones. The gist is, these nuts were looking for paths to immortality, and a lot of it included blood and sacrifice."

"Jesus. Along the lines of that blood countess ... what was her name? Elizabeth Báthory?"

"Something like that."

"That's sick."

"Yeah." Stephen leaned forward and stubbed out his cigarette. "It freaked me out, that's for sure. What's worse ... not long before *that* night, Sky left some of her toys on the living room floor and he tripped. He caught himself, but it was still enough to send him into a rage. He grabbed her by the arm and shook her. She didn't cry. She rarely did—I think she tried to copy me that way. Mama went to step in, but he let go and shoved Sky away first, mumbling something about maybe needing her later. And I didn't get the impression it was in a fuzzy, loving, Daddy kind of way. After that, he went out."

Chloe gaped at him, face going pale and a little too still.

"So, call me superstitious, but Sky going back there disturbs me a little." With that, Stephen rose to look for more cigarettes.

Chapter Seven

It wasn't quite nine on a Saturday morning and only a handful of guests were visiting the lobby for their complimentary breakfast. Sky opted for juice and a tasteless bran muffin before slipping out the front entrance. Sultry air wrapped around her, signaling the scorcher ahead and securing contentment in her decision to get out and about early. Come Monday, the semester would start and her free time would shrink to a speck.

Securing her running belt (Stephen had laughed his ass off, until she'd shown him the extra pouch for pepper spray), Skylar started at a jog and headed south toward the main drag, picking up the pace when she hung a right and proceeded west toward the university. She flew by businesses and more apartment complexes. Just across from the school, a park spread out, hugging the banks of the river with grass, punctuated with sand-filled volleyball courts and mature trees. Several buildings flanked the courts, one advertising tube rentals, seemingly a popular pastime for the area. People would float for hours, lugging an extra inner tube behind with the express purpose of holding beer and soda filled ice chests. She figured she'd have to try it sometime.

More people began appearing in the crystalline morning. Several teenagers claimed one of the volleyball courts, a family snagged a few picnic benches to begin decorating for a child's birthday party, and people with inner tubes were hitting the water.

Paying little attention, she ran aside the curves of the river, listening to the thump of her feet and the whoosh of her breath. Several inlets led down to the edge of the water, some cement with ladders, others just natural embankments inviting wading. After just a moment's hesitation, she slowed and wandered toward one, watching her step to avoid twisting an ankle in the surface roots of a nearby tree. Plopping down, she pulled off her socks and shoes and dangled her feet in the water, gasping at the chill. She'd read somewhere the temperature changed very little between winter and summer.

Hell, they hadn't been kidding.

Leaning back on locked elbows, she absently kicked her feet in the cold rush. She closed her eyes, and her mind drifted to home. If Steve drew the short straw, he'd be at the garage until twelve. If not, he'd still be in bed. Maybe Chloe would be with him (Sky hoped so. The woman was a good counterbalance for him). She even wondered what Casey was up to. They'd broken up and gone their separate ways months ago, but she couldn't help but think about him. Or perhaps it was just home in general.

The day's impending heat prickled across her skin and she sighed. It wouldn't be hard to doze off and even as the thought surfaced, her consciousness ebbed until the persistent feeling of being watched glimmered on the edge of her instincts.

Cracking an eye open, she noted a backlit figure standing over her. A sweet, but loud voice startled her.

"Hi!"

Sky sat up, blinking at the little girl. She was about seven or eight, with curly hair past her shoulders and big brown eyes. A pink hairband with a daisy kept the locks out of her face and a charm bracelet jingled from her wrist. The kid grinned at her, swinging her arms.

Amusement tugged at the corner of her mouth. Generally, Sky liked kids. "Hi, yourself."

"You have to be careful so close to the water. If

you fell in, that could be disastrous." The little girl nodded along with her own assessment.

"I suppose it could." Skylar smiled into the girl's sparkling eyes. "I'll keep that in mind. Thank you."

"You're welcome."

"Avi!" A baritone called out from the rim of trees and the girl turned.

"I'm here, Daddy! I might have saved a lady's life!"

Skylar chuckled and pulled her feet from the water, giving them a half-assed shake to dispel droplets. She wriggled back into her socks and running shoes.

"You know I don't want you too close to the water without me."

"I wasn't *that* close."

A tall, broad-shouldered man appeared beside the little girl, resting a hand protectively on her shoulder. Dark waves curled just over his ears, framing an angular, attractive face. Friendly blue-grey eyes peered down at her from beneath a crinkled brow.

The little girl looked up and beamed at him.

"Are you bothering this lady?" He stared at Sky for a long moment, face making a slow shift from relaxed to uncertain. Blinking, his mouth quirked to the side, stopping before it could be considered a full smile. "I'm sorry if she's being a pest."

"She's fine and she wasn't too close to the water." Unsure how to read the semblance of a smile that no longer reached his eyes, Sky turned her attention back to the little girl reaching to shake her hand. "Thanks for the safety tip. I'm Skylar and it's very nice to meet you."

"I'm Avery and my dad is Jack."

****

Jack greeted the woman with a nod, startled by the sudden flip in his belly.

What the hell?

It was the same woman he'd almost knocked down the stairs a few weeks back.

The woman's turquoise tank top, damp with perspiration, clung to her upper body. The slim line of a bra strap peeked from under the top and he took note of the shape of her breasts before catching himself. Her long blonde hair was pulled back in a ponytail, but several strands had come loose to dance in front of her nose. Her skin was flushed from sun or exercise, expression curious. Those same almond eyes—so blue they bordered on violet—gazed up at him and Jack felt that familiar, yet long dormant stirring deep inside. It had seemed harmless to check her out in that earlier fleeting moment, but now discomfort curdled inside. He met the woman's gaze for a moment before looking down at her outstretched hand. He took it in his, finding her grip firm, skin soft.

"I apologize, but my kid has a habit of getting me into these situations."

"Situations?" Skylar tilted her head slightly to the right, a half-smile forming on her full lips.

"Invading someone's space and pretending she doesn't have *ulterior* motives." He glanced down at his daughter, narrowing his eyes.

"I don't do that!" The girl giggled even as she denied the accusation.

"What about your friend Jennifer's mom at the grocery store?"

"I just said she was nice." Avery giggled again.

"And the cashier at the gas station."

"She had cool hair. It was orange and spiked."

"The UPS lady?"

"She had a tattoo on her wrist."

Jack shook his head, exasperated, amused, and a

little disconcerted. It had been a very long time since he'd had such an attraction to a stranger. The last time was when he'd plopped down at a bus stop next to a curly haired woman with a great smile. Guilt stole in when Nikki's image sifted into his consciousness. He knew he had no reason to feel guilty, but it reared up and pushed its claws into him regardless. Besides, just like before, he was reacting strictly to the way this woman looked. She could very well suck as a person and he didn't have time for that. "Well, I'm sorry we disturbed your peace. C'mon kiddo. We've got some errands to do before it gets too hot."

"I don't wanna go to the hardware store," the girl grumbled, pinching her face into a theatrical frown.

The woman looked from father to child and back again. "How old is she?"

"Usually eight, sometimes fifteen, very occasionally, forty-two."

Skylar gave him a brilliant smile, a throaty laugh bubbling over. "Fairly certain my brother said the same about me when I was around her age."

Staring at her for longer than he should, he pulled his gaze away with effort and refocused on Avery. "Okay, munchkin, let's go. I'm sure the nice lady has things to do to."

"I guess." The girl mumbled, staring down at the toes of her sandals.

Jack managed to meet Skylar's eyes one more time. "It was nice meeting you."

"Likewise."

Without another word, he wrapped an arm around his daughter's shoulders and guided her toward the bridge and the parking lot beyond. He tried not to pay attention when Avery twisted around more than once to wave goodbye to the woman.

His instincts claimed she most likely didn't suck as a person.

Chapter Eight

Amused, Sky waved back to the little girl. *Cute guy, cute kid.*

Oddly enough, the guy seemed familiar. She just couldn't place him.

She allowed her gaze to slide down the man's lean form, how he now held his daughter's hand before dropping it and looping an arm around the child's shoulders again. He pulled her close and kissed the top of her head, smiling.

The girl smiled back at him.

He puzzled her a little, but the interplay between father and daughter touched her. She vaguely wondered about the girl's mother, but batted it aside. It wasn't her business.

Sky sighed, looked away from Avery and "her dad, Jack," and glanced around her surroundings, considering her choices.

Without overthinking, she left the park behind at a moderate run and chose to head farther south to complete the circle back to the hotel. She passed by the main entrance of the university, small independent businesses, and chain restaurants, before beginning to make random turns, concentrating on her pace and listening to her footfalls.

Her brain filled with white noise and she found rare peace within. All her tenacious worries loosened and drifted, lost in the euphoric rush of heart and breath.

The neighborhood she entered closed around her in the lush shade of mature trees. She passed impressive stately homes, tiny bungalows, modest ranch style houses, Victorians, and cute craftsman. People of all ages were watering their lawns, weeding gardens, washing cars, or just relaxing on their front porches.

She made another turn, finding herself heading into a dead-end street. She followed the curve as it guided her around and down the other side. Her pace slowed and she came to a stop before a home built within the cute craftsman style she'd admired on previous streets.

Hedges lined a path leading to a wide, covered front porch bracketed by pillars anchored in stone. A dormer with a small single paned window jutted from above low eaves, centered over a front door accented with beveled glass. The long driveway adjacent to the home led back to a one-car detached garage with a dense greenbelt beyond. A huge elm tree took up residence in the front yard, shielding the home and shadowing the adjacent street.

It was a pretty little house, painted turquoise with white trim, more reminiscent of a seaside abode than something smack in the middle of Texas hill country.

Unsure why she stopped, she continued to stare at it.

Maybe it was because of the color. Most every other home opted for more earthy tones. This house seemed to sparkle. Capiz shell wind chimes hung just to the side of the front door and a seagrass mat welcomed dirty shoes.

A guttural call from above made Sky tilt her head upward. The shadows of several ravens passed over her and unease slid over her, skin tight and cloying. Swallowing, she looked back at the house just as all the color bled away, revealing a bone white structure and dark, gaping windows. Weeds grew in tufts against the base of the house, some stretching out tendrils to creep over the open shutters of the first floor. The lawn had been mowed, but in haste. Wheat colored grass congealed in dry patches. Near the base of the tree with its skeletal limbs hanging in mock threat, a stuffed dog had been deserted. One of its plastic eyes dangled over its nappy cheek.

Just beyond one window of the house, movement shifted, fluttered, somehow darker against the blackness, oily, waiting. Beckoning.

Sky felt as if she were falling, deep inside her mind, chest, and belly. The sidewalk remained firm beneath her feet, but they'd become rooted, pulling her down through the concrete and into the earth.

****

Molly sat at the table, sipping orange spice tea and nibbling on a lemon scone. Mr. Chuckles had already eaten his breakfast, but now sat a few feet away, pretending he wasn't watching her, expression cautiously optimistic. Knowing she shouldn't, she broke off a piece of scone and tossed it to the dog.

He inhaled it midair and grinned his happy dog grin at her.

"You're welcome, ya big goof."

His heavy tail thumped the wooden floor.

Molly took another nibble of her scone and peered out the window. She enjoyed watching the grackles frolicking in the front yard. It always amused her when spring rolled around and the males strutted their stuff. Most of the females would size them up for a few moments and then fly away. They were a capricious lot.

Instead of grackles, a girl stood on the sidewalk in front of the neighbor's house. Her hands hung to her sides, her face blank, pale. She appeared to sway.

Concern lanced through her and she lurched to her feet and out the front door. Chuck followed behind in case she needed assistance.

The girl hadn't moved. She was older than Molly originally thought. Late 20s maybe? Long blonde hair was pulled back in a tail. Sweat glistened against her brow and darkened her tank top.

"Darlin', are you alright? You look like you just stared the devil in the eye!"

Jumping as if zapped by a power line, a moment of panicked wildness crossed the young woman's face and settled in her eyes. She whirled toward Molly. "*What?*"

Molly swallowed a gasp and managed not to step back. The girl's eyes merged blue with violet, striking and a little unnerving. She'd only seen that particular shade of color once, and she hadn't liked the person they'd belonged to.

"*What?*" The blonde woman repeated, panic ebbing into confusion.

"Honey, you looked like you were in a trance." Molly lowered her voice to soothe, despite her own shock. "Are you all right? Is there someone I should call?"

Maybe something popped in the kid's head. You could never predict these things.

Silence answered Molly's question for a few long moments, before the girl blinked several times, as if awakening from a particularly nasty nightmare. "Um … no. No, I'm fine. Thank you." She managed a smile, tentative at first, but it quickly reached those scary, gorgeous eyes, warming them.

Molly relaxed.

Mr. Chuckles nudged the girl's hand and her smile widened. She stroked the dog's broad head. "He's beautiful."

"Thank you. He's also a great judge of character. I'm Molly Achen and this is Mr. Chuckles. Or Chuck. He answers to either." Molly looped her arm through the young woman's "And you are?"

"Skylar." She glanced back at the house and a brief frown creased her brow. She looked away. "I apologize for that. I don't know what happened. I just kind of spaced out."

"Mmhm." Molly once more paused at the name. Skylar. Was that even *possible*? "Well, it seems you're okay now, but just in case, can I offer you some lemonade or sweet tea? Come on in out of the heat for a few minutes. Chuck and I would love the company."

The girl hesitated but only for a moment. "Sure, thank you. I'd like that."

****

Skylar let the woman lead her next door. Molly chattered in good-nature and Sky enjoyed the relaxed, matter of fact way she spoke. Her manner calmed her down, taking her away from that awful feeling she'd just experienced and didn't want to spend time contemplating. At least, not right now. She guessed the woman to be in her mid-sixties, an aging hippy wearing a long, beaded tunic, yoga pants, and bare feet. An anklet looped around just above her right foot. She wore her white hair past her shoulders with several narrow braids woven within.

Chuck followed, nudging Sky for more pets, which she was happy to give him. She scratched the top of his head lightly.

The little house was all rich wood, beads, and patchouli. Just beyond the entry in the front room, Sky spotted an easel and dozens of canvases leaning against the walls.

"I'm not very good, but I enjoy painting anyhow," Molly commented, guiding her to the right and through the kitchen to the breakfast nook "Have a seat."

Remnants of a meal disturbed littered the table and a pang of guilt resounded inside. The sidewalk where they'd just stood was readily visible. "I'm sorry I pulled you from your breakfast."

"Nonsense." Molly waved a hand and Skylar sat on the bench seat. "Chuck and I were chilling. We just got home from a road trip last week. We spent six months with my daughter up north. Now we're happily home to exist without her dour face scrutinizing everything."

Sky blinked, unsure how to respond.

"It's okay, you can smile if you think it's funny. I love her to pieces, but she's always looking for a reason to keep me under her thumb. Thinks I'm going senile."

"I don't see that at all." Sky responded in truth.

"Thank you. Neither do I. So, Skylar, what happened out there? Are you really okay?"

Molly placed a glass of tea before her and Sky smiled in gratitude. She took a sip, trying not to wince at the liberal amount of sugar. "Yes, I think so. Just one of those things. Too much stress, I guess."

Molly watched her with sharp green eyes. "You from around here? Your accent is not quite local, but similar. But then again, what do I know? I haven't exactly studied sociolinguistics."

"Well, kind of. I was born down here, but left when I was very small. To be honest, I have very few memories. I actually grew up in Oklahoma."

"I see." Molly nodded, as if confirming something to herself. "So, you back to stay?"

"Maybe. I'm teaching at the university. Anthropology, specializing in Native American studies." Sky glanced down when her phone buzzed, but made no move to check it. Mawmaw would never have approved.

"Wow. Impressive. I'm lucky I earned an

Associate. I'm more of a life learner, myself. What are the odds that you'd return to your birthplace to teach? I mean, it's not exactly a huge town."

A shadow passed through Sky's mind, the odd feeling of falling inside tormenting her in recent memory. She fought a shudder. "Impossible, so you'd think."

Chapter Nine

Jack's first thought between his sleepless night and the shrill blaring of the alarm clock, was that he should simply just call in. No questions. No frowns of concern. No long looks from the few who knew.

But his schedule was packed. There were too many appointments in his capacity as associate dean to shoulder off to another colleague, and both his classes were already expecting feedback on short narratives they'd been assigned on Monday. Jack had never been one to waste the first week of the semester, but now regretted the compulsion. Some of his students wrote in a perfunctory way, while others used words as art. It was easy to tell the difference between those who did it because they had to and those who wrote for love. Not that all who wrote for love were good, but they tried despite the awkwardness.

No. He couldn't bail on the day. It wouldn't be fair to anyone, least of all, himself. Too much time alone would lead to too much conjecture and wallowing. It was best to keep busy, exhaustion and self-pity be damned.

He watched the room grow a little lighter, knowing he needed to get up, his mind and body doing their best to inhibit him.

Two years ago today. Two years ago, Nikki had kissed him and Avery goodbye, gone off to her volunteer gig, and never came back.

The weight of loss pressed him down, suffocating in its power. Only when he heard his daughter stirring did he manage to kick the blanket and sheet off and swing his legs over the edge of the bed.

"Hi, Daddy!" Avery appeared in the doorway, her feet silent on the thick carpet of the bedroom. She dove at him for her morning cuddle, oblivious to the black hole he was swimming in. Her memory of the day had long dimmed and he was thankful.

"Good morning, baby." Jack held her close for a moment, the scent of very-berry shampoo in his nose.

"What are you doing today?" She bounced around, happy in her morning person abilities.

"The usual."

"Do you think we'll ever run into Skylar again?" She continued to bounce on the bed.

Jack blanked. "*Who*?"

"The lady at the park."

"Um. I don't know. I doubt it." He wasn't sure if he hoped to run into her again or not. Guilt was a thorny bitch.

Her face fell. "Oh. She was a nice lady and pretty."

He pulled in a deep breath. "Yeah, I guess she was."

Stopping, Avery stared up at the ceiling, contemplating. Growing serious, she chewed on her lower lip. "Daddy?"

"Hmmm?"

"Would you ever get married again?"

The chill sliced deep and painful. "I don't know. Why?"

"My friend Ashleigh's mom just got married, so she got a new dad. I'm not sure what happened to the first one … I think he went missing or something. But the new one's name is Ted."

"Niña bonita! Breakfast!"

Avery spun around without pause and galloped from the room, following the voice of her nanny, Rosa, and the aroma of bacon.

Jack stared after her. *Of all the damned days.*

With a deep sigh, he pushed off the edge of the bed to shuffle toward the shower.

****

Skylar hung out after class, chatting with students and fielding questions. At least a dozen approached her, from anything regarding individual conferences to preparation for the final project almost twelve weeks down the road. Those particular folks alternately impressed and appalled her, and she wasn't sure what that said about her as a professor.

Despite the countless hours she'd served as a TA and the equally countless hours she'd worked in the field alongside students and faculty alike, the idea of teaching five classes and over one hundred and twenty people teetered on overwhelming her. She hid the impulse to slip away behind a veneer of self-confidence she didn't always feel.

When the last student sifted away, Sky peeked at her phone. She'd held onto her brother's text from last week. His first contact since she'd left was very *him*.

Stephen: **Hey, geek. How are things? Good luck in the big leagues.**

And like that, everything was good between them again. She wondered if it was Benny or Chloe who kicked his ass. Probably a little of both. Maybe Mawmaw's spirit even stopped by to chastise him. She sure as hell would have done it in life.

She packed up her briefcase and laptop, startling at the sudden voice from the doorway.

"Well, professor, now that you're at the top of your third week, how is it going?"

Sky looked up, smiling at her colleague. Dr. Elise Brown had been on the hiring committee, seeing exuberance and passion where some only saw inexperience. The woman may not have been directly responsible for her offer, but had no doubt weighed heavily in favor of it. Long tenured, Elise was a stout, eccentric woman in her upper 50's, with blue tinted hair. Sky had liked her on sight.

"Um, not too bad. I've assisted in classes loads during my grad work, but flying free, well, it's definitely more intense. Getting my sea legs, so to speak."

"I bet. Just be careful. Throw some chum in and the sharks will circle."

Her heavy frown at the metaphor spurred laughter from the other woman.

"I mean, don't let them smell blood. If they think you don't have it together, they'll try to take advantage. Or at least challenge you."

"Not just the kids." A student ten years or so her senior had told her she didn't look old enough to be have a bachelor's degree, let alone, a doctorate. She'd just smiled, telling him she'd worked her ass off and never slept. Not exactly a fabrication.

"True enough. People are people. Just don't let them rattle you. And if they do, don't let it show."

"I can hold my own. Most have been fine. What's odd though is I still have people trying to add my classes. It's kind of nuts." Students had through week two of the semester to fine tune their schedules, most of the insanity taking place the first day. By the third week, everything was set.

Elise stared at her for a hard moment before throwing back her head and howling with laughter. The woman reined herself in as Sky watched her, puzzled. "Honey, when was the last time you looked in the mirror?"

Sky rolled her eyes. "That's ridiculous."

The woman just smiled. "Not to a nineteen-year-old. Of course, we have a few other professors with the same problem on campus. If you want to call it a problem." She grabbed Sky's arm and walked out of the classroom with her. "By the way, did anyone tell you about the staff retreat?"

"Retreat? What is that? Some kind of weekend thing?"

"Nope. Just a less formal lounge with a better view. It's a good choice if you need to get away." Elise nudged her to the left. "Trust me."

"Um … okay…"

"I have an appointment to get to, but I just wanted to take a moment to show you while I thought about it." Elise pushed through the metal door at end of the hallway to enter the stairwell. Instead of going down, she pointed up toward an exit marked, 'No Admittance. Alarm will sound.' "Don't pay attention to that. Just try to go up here when there aren't any students around."

She led Sky up a short flight of stairs and pushed through the door warning of immediate regret. It led into a small dim alcove, and Elise made another right and exited into the bright afternoon.

A concrete patio spread out before them, leading to a four-foot-high perimeter barrier, and beyond it, views of the entire town. Intrigued, Sky stepped up to the wall, leaning into it and absorbing house rooftops, distant historical buildings, greenbelts lining the river, and the passing train to the east. Clear, brilliant blue skies and fluffy cumulous clouds rounded out the postcard view. "It's lovely."

"It is. It also appears we're not the only ones to enjoy this beautiful view today. Hello, Jack. How are you?"

Skylar turned at the same time Elise greeted a man who'd been leaning against the southern side. She'd been so overtaken with the view she hadn't even noticed they weren't alone. Locking eyes with him, she sucked in a breath.

The man from that day at the park.

He seemed just as startled to see her before his expression closed in on itself. Turning his attention to the older woman, he managed a weak smile. "Not too bad, Elise. I hope everything is good with you and Frank."

"Absolutely. He's already planning a trip to Spain for us this winter break. You know how he is. The man can't sit still for long."

"I envy him."

"Yeah, so do I, until it occurs to me that I have to go along with him." She laughed long and hard before turning her attention back to Sky. "I'm so sorry. This is our resident horror author, Jack. In addition to other things of course. Hey, Jack, have you met our new Anthropology professor? Dr. Jack Langham meet Dr. Skylar Donaghue."

She took his offered hand, meeting his eyes again. They were no longer the embarrassed father, but seemed reserved, aloof. His grip was firm, but he withdrew the greeting quickly.

"Oh! I have to go. One of my students in probably getting bored waiting for me in my office." Elise hustled toward the door. "I'll see you both next week!"

Skylar gave her a wave, just as the heavy fire door slammed behind the woman. "She has a lot of energy."

Jack grunted in response and when she turned, she found him staring at her, eyes intense, their blue-grey mostly steel. Annoyance rippled through her, but she did her best to hide it. "Did I do something wrong? You look like you want to take a poke at me. Just know, I *will* fight back.

He blinked, appeared startled for a moment, before shaking his head. His rich voice sounded strained. "No, of course not."

Skylar narrowed her eyes, recognition seeping in. "That day in the Main Hall before the semester started. You were the guy on the stairs."

"I suppose I was."

Silence filled the vacuum between them before the man cleared his throat. "I need to leave as well. It was nice to see you again."

The tone of his voice said different and he left without waiting for any acknowledgement, the heavy door banging shut behind him.

Confused and irritated, Sky stared after him before trying to shake it off. The guy obviously had issues. Whether the real man was the attractive, embarrassed father from the park or the indifferent jerk who just left, it was anyone's guess.

She turned back toward the town where she'd made such a large move, mood shifting. Several minutes before she'd seen something quaint, even sweet. Now parts of it looked old, in crumbling disrepair.

Of course, it was just a town like anywhere else.

A dark silhouette drifted above her for a moment before landing on the wall several feet from her. The raven hopped along the stone, stopping to tilt its head toward her. One shining eye appeared to size her up.

All thoughts of Jack Langham and the recent move disappeared and she stared at the bird, a chill settling into her bones.

It hopped a little closer, cawing in its strangled vocals.

"Go away." The words stuck in her throat, releasing in a weak trickle.

She felt stupid. It was just a bird. Superstition

should have been negated by education, but like many Choctaw, she often wandered in that nebulous spot where culture, upbringing, and schooling intersected. It was an uneasy mix.

The incident outside that house came back and flooded over her. She shivered in the heat.

Skylar tried again, cold and agitated at the raven's proximity, but warming her anger. "Get lost!"

This time her words had more power, startling the bird. It cawed again and seemed to shoot her an accusatory look before taking flight and disappearing from view.

Chapter Ten

Jack made the turn and pulled into his driveway, cutting the ignition. It was still early, light pushing from his home into the new darkness. Remaining still for several minutes, his mind raced with memories, anger, and emotional fatigue. He'd been stuck in his own self-imposed prison for so long, he didn't know how to scratch his way out.

And now there'd been three chance meetings, and he'd be damned if he could get her out of his head.

Dr. Skylar Donaghue.

He'd felt the immediate draw that first day and didn't think much about it beyond his hormones. Then there was the park. Jack figured the likelihood of ever seeing her again ended right there. Then it turned out she taught at the university as well. What were the odds?

The attraction wasn't wrong. After two years of being a widower, it couldn't be, but then why the hell did he feel so damned guilty?

Guilt or no guilt, he knew one thing. At the very least he owed the woman an apology.

Now he just needed to burn everything off. He'd worry about the apology later.

He hopped out of the truck, bypassed the little gate leading toward the house, and let himself into the garage, flipping on the overhead. Just to the right, a bookshelf system nestled within its wooden confines. He didn't remember what CD was in there, but it didn't matter. He just wanted something to help him cleanse his mind. Tapping the 'on' button, the sounds of 90's grunge filled the small garage.

Stripping to his t-shirt, he tossed the button down across a storage tote, toed off his shoes and socks, and stepped toward the middle of his makeshift gym. He dropped to the mat and started with pushups, going until his arms burned and he'd lost count. He followed with crunches before bouncing to his feet and reaching for gloves.

A freestanding training bag beckoned, and he released all his pent-up anger and frustration with a series of hits hard enough to rock the two-hundred-and-fifty-pound base.

Sweat burned his eyes, almost blinding him, but he persisted, his breath rasping, his lungs complaining, and exhaustion threatening to take him down in a header to the mat.

Hit after hit, he expelled every bit of feeling, hoping for numbness, unsure to his success. Intense focus and loud music kept him from hearing the tiny voice at the door.

The music abruptly ceased.

"*Daddy?*"

Jack swiveled, unsteady as his body trembled from fatigue, irritation flowing outward. "Avi, *what* are you doing out here?"

She bit her lip, eyes rounding at his tone. "I … I saw the light. I was a little worried. Are you okay?"

Pulling air deep into his lungs, he allowed its slow release. "I'm sorry, sweetie. You just caught me off guard."

"You looked really angry."

"Not at you."

"Who, then?"

Excellent question. Who was he angry at? His dead wife? Skylar Donaghue? Himself? Yeah, that last one was a given, but he wasn't even being fair to himself at this point. Logically, he knew this. Emotionally, well, that was a tough one.

The last time he'd spoken to Avery's grandparents, his mother-in-law had come right out and asked if he was seeing anyone. It had startled him and he'd floundered for any kind of answer. Her question hadn't been an attack, just simple curiosity. When he didn't respond, her words were gentle. "I know you loved my Nikki, but it's time you let her go. You're a young man. You have your whole life before you. Avery won't be a little girl for long and you need to think of yourself."

It stung and he'd flinched from the impact. Nikki's mother had never been one to pull punches.

Now his daughter stood before him, frowning and waiting for an answer. She grew and matured every single day and if he wasn't careful, she'd be living her own life before long and he'd be left wondering what the hell happened.

"I'm okay."

Avery narrowed her eyes, unconvinced.

"You want to go a couple of rounds?"

Suspicion and worry morphed into surprise. She probably never expected to touch the bag again after hitting Andrew. "Really?"

Jack pulled off his gloves and wriggled them onto Avery's tiny hands, pulling the straps to tighten them as much as possible. They were awkward, but the little girl didn't care. She already bounced, jabbed and twirled in pretense.

"I can still hit the bag?"

"Sure. No more punching kids in school though." He tilted his head in thought. "Unless they have it coming, of course."

She smirked at him before landing several decent punches. The little girl gritted her teeth in concentration to hit even harder.

"Remember to put your weight behind it."

She did as he suggested and made a bigger impact.

"There you go!"

Grinning, she showed the new gap in her teeth, the same one that had cost him a couple of bucks several nights back.

"Try to get me." Jack circled around her, reaching out and mussing her hair in provocation.

"Hey!"

"C'mon, you can do it!"

She pursued him and he sidestepped her attempts, smiling at the dogged determination in her face. Avery wasn't the type of kid to back down from a challenge.

Jack landed a tickling finger under one armpit, and Avery swung wild at him. He bounced back out of reach, her hit flailing in air.

"No fair!"

Jack chuckled, continuing his circle. The second before she followed him, he flicked her ear and earned himself a kidney punch when she swiveled and struck out.

"Oof."

Her grin could have split the night into dawn. "Gotcha!"

Holding up his hands in surrender, he took a moment to catch his breath. "Okay, okay, I think I'm done. You took the point, so we'll call it a night."

Her eyes glistened. "Could we do this again soon?"

"Is that bloodlust I see?"

"Yup. Can we?"

"We'll see. Just don't tell Principal Daily." Jack grabbed a towel from the short storage shelf to the left of the bag and mopped his face and the back of his neck. He smiled as Avery tried without success to wriggle out of the gloves. "Come here a second."

He unlaced the gloves and tossed them near the towels. Jack swooped his daughter into his arms and planted a loud raspberry against her cheek, enjoying the sound of her giggles.

He still wasn't sure if he felt better, but his little girl's happiness and his own fatigue were a good start. With any luck, the exhaustion would lead to a much-needed dreamless slumber.

Chapter Eleven

"Calling Dr. D, calling Dr. D!" A head poked into the meeting room where Sky held her last class.

She smiled at the man even though he served as a mild irritant. Emerson Fanning was Dr. Brown's assistant, and Sky only hoped she'd been less annoying when she'd held the same capacity for Dr. Feinstein during her doctoral pursuit. "Hi, Emerson. What can I do for you?"

"I've been instructed, via doctors Brown, Skellen, and Taylor, and Mr. Demming, Douglas, and Ms. Campshaw, that your appearance is requested at The Pub this evening." He grinned, showing every one of his impressively large teeth. "I've been told that 'no' is not an acceptable answer unless it's attached to hospitalization or a trip to Paris."

"I don't think…"

"You know they're going to just keep pestering you." He waggled his eyebrows.

Every Friday they tried to rein her in, and every Friday she'd managed to avoid the inevitable. Her plans for the evening had included relaxation with a good book and maybe grading some papers, which oozed depression.

God, when had she gotten old?

Maybe a night out was what she needed. Perhaps she'd sleep better. Before she could think better of it, she smiled at him again. "Sure. When should I be there?"

****

Jack hated this crap. This was a huge mistake. He should never have agreed to come.

He'd had the misfortune to boot a student out of the university that afternoon, and Hal Hendersen, a meek-looking fifty-something-year-old adviser with thick oval glasses, had popped his head into his office. His watery, myopic eyes had fixed on Jack and 'encouraged' him to join everyone for Friday night festivities. It would be a good way to forget his crap day.

In a moment of poor decision, Jack had figured, sure, why not. Some distraction couldn't be a bad thing.

Now, the room overflowed with buzzing voices, loud guffaws, and bass from pedestrian pop music. It all bounced off ornate walls nodding to Texas's illustrious past and landed within the perimeters of his skull. The vibration blocked most access to his own thoughts, and he rubbed one temple in a fruitless attempt to quell a budding headache.

Hal slapped him on the shoulder and yelled something. Jack wasn't positive, but it sounded like, "See? All you needed was a hopping bar to forget about a shitty day." Or words to that effect. The strong scent of a eucalyptus cough drop accompanied the comment, and Jack winced and recoiled.

The man didn't appear to notice. Hal liked to go out and used any excuse to do so. This particular occasion revolved around Jack's bad day. Of course, the invitation included another assistant dean, two more advisers, and one administrator.

The bar stood less than a half mile from the campus, nestled in the oldest part of the business district. It was frequented by faculty, staff, and the occasional intrepid student. Jack had avoided the place until now, but a questionable day coupled with lack of judgment had gotten the best of him.

"You did the right thing. You know that, right?" Hal yelled. This time, in the beat between songs, Jack heard him.

The fact he'd kicked a student out of the

university that afternoon was just a portion of what was on his mind. A very small portion. He'd spent the last couple of weeks volleying between paging through old albums of his dead wife and having waking dreams of Skylar Donaghue. He'd only seen her one other time since acting like an ass to her at the rooftop retreat. She'd been in the library speaking with a couple of students, dressed in another skirt and blouse, her hair pinned up as before. He couldn't help but wonder what it would look like out of pins, out of a ponytail, and cascading over her shoulders and down her back. When a smile lit up her face during her conversation, he'd left with a pain in his belly.

His Texas porter warmed in front of him and he debated excuses to leave. Usually, Avery was his go-to reason, but she was spending the night with a friend and he was, no doubt, the last thing on her mind. He would have been replaced by another giggling girl, ponies, kittens, and a Chihuahua named Pete.

Lily, the admin, leaned over, caressing his bicep with one well-manicured index finger. Her perfume cloying, make-up a little too thick, the woman was pushing forty and kicking and screaming the whole way. "Have any plans for tomorrow night? I know of a great party if you'd like to pop by."

Her lips remained by his ear and he could have sworn she deliberately blew inside. Jack liked her; he really did. She was a very sweet person, but a recent divorce and too many scotch and sodas pushed the sweet back in favor of the obnoxious.

"Taking my daughter to the movies."

"Well, afterward, when the little one is tucked away, the adults can go out and play." She laughed at her own wit and he smiled in response.

"I'll think about it."

"Don't think too hard." Her hand dropped and she traced up his thigh with those long nails.

Jack jumped and hit the table. If it hadn't been there, he might have found himself hanging from one of the exposed wooden beams above. Being groped by a co-worker hadn't been on the list of expectations for the night. He could only imagine how Lily was going to feel after she'd slept off her alcohol-induced explorative tendencies. Poor woman.

Lurching to his feet, he smiled down into her perplexed eyes. "Sorry. Men's room."

The smile melted from his face, leaving tightness behind. If he bolted, it might make him look bad, but he could always claim illness. It wouldn't even be that much of a stretch. The place was getting to him. Too many people, too much craziness. He needed quiet so he could form one rational thought. What that thought might be, he wasn't sure, but he wanted the option at least.

Jack pivoted to weave his way through the crowd and toward the back hallway.

****

The restaurant/bar took its place in a connecting series of historical buildings, right across the street from the well-manicured lawns of the old courthouse. With distressed brick walls and open beams, it should have been cozy, but missed the opportunity with too much lighting and tables. Skylar didn't see a single booth to hide in.

Not that she would have been allowed to. She was caught in a wave of colleagues that propelled her forward into The Pub's cacophony. Although early, some folks already appeared besotted and her discomfort soared. She didn't drink, so on the rare occasions she went out, she was often stuck with designated driver duty.

There were eight in their group and they herded over to snag a couple of tables on the east side of the bar, directly under a collection of vintage tin signs, advertising Valvoline, Jack Daniels, and Harley-Davidson, among others. Sky managed to find a seat with her back to the wall, filling an instinct she'd had all her life.

"So, what do you think?" Emerson leaned in from her right, and she wished he'd back away.

"Loud."

"It'll get louder." He laughed. "Educators can be nuts after a long week dealing with whining students. But you probably know that."

She shrugged, her experience varying.

His big teeth glinted in the light before he edged close enough for her to feel his breath against her ear. "Can I grab you something, Dr. D? Or can I call you Skylar?"

"Thank you, but I'll get it." Ignoring his question, she scooted her chair out, leaving him staring after her. There was no way in hell that she'd allow someone she barely knew to bring her a drink.

She crossed to the bar, weaving around too many people in too small a space.

Smoothing her skirt over her hips, Sky perched on the edge of a bar stool, feeling a little exposed when she couldn't press her back to a corner. Trying not to think about it, her gaze roamed everywhere, noting the colorful collection of bottles behind the counter, as well as a couple dozen spigots for beer on tap. Shelves above were crowded with trinkets and figurines—Buddha statues, bronze goblets, one figure of the Hindu God Ganesh, a cow skull, several old-fashioned lanterns, dozens of ceramic and pewter animals, and one stuffed jungle cat as a nod to the school mascot. It was an eccentric mess but she liked its brazen sensibilities.

"What can I get for you?" The bartender grinned, exposing late-life braces.

"Cranberry and Sprite."

"You got it."

He returned with her drink a moment later and set it before her.

She took a sip, relishing the tang, and swiveled on the stool to stand just in time to see Jack Langham emerge from the back hallway. His hair was mussed into dark disheveled waves, his tie pulled down and sleeves rolled up to expose lean and powerful arms. She caught a glimpse of a small tattoo she hadn't noticed before. Slight shadows pressed beneath his eyes, and it occurred to her she wasn't the only one who hadn't slept well last night.

When he looked up, they made eye contact and an instantaneous tremor ran through her, bringing gooseflesh to the surface. An odd fusing of irritation and attraction twisted inside. The man was an odd bird. She'd sensed interest that day in the park, even as he'd struggled with his daughter's adorable attempt to match make, but that day on the roof terrace? He'd been flat out rude.

She wondered which man currently gazed back at her.

Langham hesitated before coming to some kind of internal decision and heading her way. His tense expression eased ever so slightly, and she soon found herself looking up at him. He must have stood over six feet, making him at least eight inches taller than she was. Even with her heels, she felt short.

"Dr. Langham." She raised her voice to be heard above the din. It sounded a little clipped to her own ears, but she figured she had the right.

"Dr. Donaghue." He stepped closer, leaning down. Spicy aftershave wafted over her with the movement. "May I speak to you outside for a moment?"

She glanced toward the front door, debated before nodding. A patio with a snarl of iron fencing wrapped around it provided limited tables for folks who didn't mind the unpredictable Texas weather.

Langham waved her before him, walking close but not touching her.

The door thumped shut behind them, cutting the noise in half. Only a handful of people sat on the patio, quiet over their drinks. Langham guided her to a corner table, watching without comment when she sat with her back to the outside wall of the bar.

She placed her drink before her but didn't take a sip. "May I ask you something?"

"Sure."

"Which Jack Langham am I currently speaking to? The helpful guy on the stairs—by the way, I *know* you were looking at my butt—or Avery's embarrassed father? Or are you the rude guy on the rooftop terrace?"

He allowed a heavy sigh, eyes downcast. "I owe you an apology. I was way out of line."

Sky didn't respond, waiting.

"That day happened to be a … hard one for me. It know it doesn't excuse my behavior. I *was* a bit of a jerk."

"Yeah, you were."

His smile looked rueful and he stared down at his hands. It faded when he gazed back at her. "I know. I'm sorry for that, but I hope you can understand a little. It happened to be the anniversary of my wife's death, so, well, I wasn't in the best frame of mind."

Blinking, Skylar felt as if an anvil had dropped in her belly. "Oh my God. I'm so sorry." Even as the words slid out, they sounded lame, inadequate. "I had no idea."

"How could you?" He continued, as if looking for atonement in honesty. "It's been two years. In some ways it seems longer, other ways, not so much."

"You don't have to explain. It's okay. I understand. You had a right to be upset."

"No, you don't understand, not yet at least." Langham watched her for a long moment, before his face pinched in apparent discomfort. He pushed ahead, holding her gaze. "The coincidences have been a bit much. That day in the main hall, and yeah, I was looking at your butt—sorry about that. Then there was the park with my daughter, the terrace. It's been a long time, so I honestly wasn't prepared to be attracted to another woman. How's that for blunt honesty?"

Warmth flowed over and through her, but all she could manage was a soft, "Oh."

Chapter Twelve

Jack wasn't sure exactly what he expected, but the woman's subdued response wasn't it. Maybe it should have been. Her eyes had widened and now she studied his face, waiting for him to continue. Or not.

That was okay though. He'd spent the last several weeks alternately brooding and kicking himself before deciding to take a tiny step forward. Since he'd already no doubt humiliated himself again, he figured he may as well go for broke.

"So, um. Well, I'm not good at this. Like I said, it's been a long time. But Avery and I would be delighted if you'd join us tomorrow night. It's nothing fancy, but we were just heading out to the drive-in for mediocre food and hopefully at least one good movie."

She stared at him.

"I'm sorry. That was kind of abrupt," he conceded, a little concerned he'd pushed too soon.

"There's an actual honest-to-God drive-in movie theater around here?"

Her intrigued tone made him relax a little. "Down the interstate just a bit."

A slow smile began in her magnificent eyes and took over her entire face. For the first time in over a decade, Jack wanted to kiss a woman who wasn't Nicole. But he'd also watched as she'd made a point to sit with her back to a wall and figured he wasn't the only one with scars.

The smile disappeared into wistfulness. "I'd love to, but I can't. Moving day tomorrow. I'll be up to my eyes in boxes the whole weekend."

"Moving day?"

"I've been living at the extended stay over a

month now. I finally got around to finding a place." She took a sip of her drink. "To be honest, I'm a little excited. All the stuff I've had in storage in Durant is making its way down to me. Finally."

"Well, you still need to eat, right? If you don't mind my kiddo, we can swoop by, pick you up, grab some burgers, and have you back in time to tackle your box avalanche." He paused, his gaze darting to the side before his smile turned slightly sheepish. "Well, the place I'm thinking also has chicken and meatless burgers, if that's more your thing. Avery makes me get the meatless one every other time."

She burst out laughing. "Your very own Jiminy Cricket."

"That's a couple words for it." He crumpled his face into a frown, but tried to keep some laughter in his eyes. "So, what do you think?"

"Sure. I'd like that."

He grinned back at her. "Good. And Avery is going to be ecstatic."

"She's a cute kid."

"Thanks." He looked around. "Did you want to stay for a little longer, or can I walk you to your car. To be honest, coming here wasn't exactly my idea."

Sky laughed again and he decided he could keep on listening to the musical sound the rest of the night. "Same here. I was kind of hoodwinked myself."

"Not the bar going type?"

"Never. I was always dragged along as the designated driver when I was in grad school. I guess I was convenient that way." She sipped her drink and his gaze drifted to her lips before he could stop himself. He tore his eyes away when she looked up. "I think I am ready to go."

Jack nodded. He'd been ready to go the moment

he stepped inside, less so when he'd been sitting outside with her. "Parked in their postage stamp lot or on the street?"

"Street."

They both rose and drifted toward the sidewalk, leaving the cacophony of the bar behind. Bright moonlight lit their path but lengthened the surrounding shadows. From the top of the old courthouse across the street, birds called out to one another in repetitive squawks.

The delicate scent of her perfume reached him and Jack shoved his hands in his pockets as he walked beside her, stifling the impulse to touch her.

"Here it is." Skylar unlocked a small blue Toyota SUV remotely and turned around to face Jack. "I'm glad we were able to talk. It felt good to clear the air."

"Same here. I'm sorry again. I usually try not to be a jerk. Well, most of the time."

"I think you had good reason." Her vibrant eyes locked on his and it took him a long moment to find his breath.

"Never an excuse to take it out on someone else. You didn't deserve that."

"No, I didn't, but I forgive you." She rested a hand on his arm and stretched up to brush his cheek with her lips.

It wouldn't have taken much to turn his head, just a moment and a couple of inches. The impulse propelled tension through his entire body, but he managed to lock down his instinctive response, smiling at her when she pulled away.

"Good night."

"Night, Skylar." He watched her climb in to her vehicle and drive away.

Chapter Thirteen

Jack drove slowly, watching addresses, thankful no one was right behind him. According to GPS, Skylar's place should pop up any moment.

Avery squirmed in her booster. "Daddy, I can run faster than this. Actually, I could hop on one foot faster than this."

"Very funny."

"You know you're going to pass it anyway. You always do." Her tone was matter-of-fact.

"Such a supportive child."

She giggled and Jack shot her a mock angry expression in the rearview mirror. She giggled louder. "So, she works at the same place you do?"

"Apparently so. She teaches Anthropology."

The girl frowned, considering. "What's that?"

"It's kind of studying people, culture, origins. That sort of thing."

"Oh." She quieted for a long moment and Jack braced. "It's funny that she works where you work."

"Not really. Lots of people work there. It's a college town."

"I don't think it's that at *all*."

Jack glanced up at her again. "Really? Then what is *it*?"

"Fate."

"Excuse me?"

"Fate. It's meant to be. Bailey knows all about it. Her mom reads crystals and they tell her all kinds of stuff."

"I bet," Jack muttered, purposely pushing against the inclination to roll his eyes.

"I think you just passed the address, Daddy!"

"Of course I did," he grumbled, shaking his head. He made a U-turn when he was clear and pulled up in front of a little bungalow set back from the road. Cream-colored stucco and dark brown trim gave it a slight Tudor appearance.

"So, are you and Sky gonna get married?"

"Avi, I barely know her." He looked up, narrowing his eyes at his presumptuous daughter. "And if you bring it up in her company, I'll hide your Shopkins and eat all your Danimals."

"But, you don't like Danimals!"

"I'll make an exception."

Jack climbed from the driver's seat and waited for Avery to release herself from the seat belt. The neighborhood felt hushed and he figured most folks were probably out and about to enjoy the warm day. Somewhere up the street, the buzz of a weed whacker cut the quiet for a couple of moments before fading. Beyond the little house, he heard the gentle flow of the river.

Fake cowhide purse swinging from her arm, Avery skipped up the path to ring the doorbell.

Jack stepped onto the porch the second the door opened.

"Hi. C'mon in for a minute. I kind of lost track of time." Sky smiled and backed away to allow them entrance. "Sorry about the ... well, you know how moving is. I forgot I had so many things."

"It's like a city in here!" Avery gasped, staring at the sea of cardboard. "It would be cool to let a cat loose in here. He or she would have a blast. Maybe you could get one."

"Umm…" The woman watched as the little girl threaded her way through the stacks of boxes.

Jack barely glanced around him. Sky wore her hair pulled back under a bandana, a loose denim shirt, rolled to her elbows, faded jeans, and red Converse sneakers. Despite understandably looking a little tired and the smudge of dust on her right cheek, she was one of the most beautiful things he'd ever seen.

He must have stared longer than he realized because pink tinged her face. Jack cleared his throat. "Sorry, I think we might be a little early. The kiddo was getting hungry."

"Uh uh. No, Dad, that was you, even though you ate three pieces of the neighbor lady's banana bread." Avery corrected him, weaving through the aisles between the cardboard stacks toward the back slider.

"I did *not* have three pieces. I had two." He defended himself, feeling a little silly when Sky smiled at him.

"Not that I can blame you. It was really, really good. And the lady has a cool dog." Avery peered through the glass. "Wow! You live right by the river. Oh! Look! Some people in inner tubes! Can we do that sometime?"

"Maybe, sometime," Jack called, gaze still on Skylar.

"Um, well, honestly, I'm a little hungry too. I accidentally skipped breakfast. Let me, just, um, clean up a little."

"Of course."

She turned and disappeared down the short hallway, as Jack ignored his stomach attempting to invert itself. He stared down at his shoes, trying to control his breathing.

God, what would Nikki think?

Don't be an idiot. Nikki would think you're an ass for not moving forward with your life, for yours and for Avery's sake. And she'd be right.

Sky reappeared, bandana gone, golden hair

brushed out and flowing over her shoulders, dirt smudge gone. "Sorry. I hadn't realized how scruffy I looked."

Jack wanted to say that was impossible. Instead, he said, "No need to apologize. Moving is a dirty business."

Avery wriggled between them, taking both their hands. "Are we ready? I'm starved."

Surprise fluttered over Skylar's face and Jack cocked one eyebrow down at his daughter.

She just grinned.

****

Sky watched the pulse in Jack's jaw with amusement. His expression read calm, but that little throb said it all.

Avery slowly walked toward them, all three of their fountain drinks hugged to her chest. The tip of her tongue pressed her upper lip in concentration as she slid each foot forward, unwilling to lift them.

Jack and his daughter had taken her to a restaurant which looked more like a shack than anything resembling a place to eat. Tucked behind a gas station, it stuck out from surrounding modern architecture with its weathered planks, metal corrugated roof, and signs advertising Coca Cola, Gulf, Texaco, route 66, and cigars. Bigger than it appeared, the inside surprised her with a quaint general store, ice cream bar, and a café serving not only the usual lunch fare, but a multitude of sinful looking baked goods. The outside theme of nostalgic signage décor continued across interior walls. Everywhere she looked, she saw ads for Dr. Pepper, Indian Motorcycles, and John Deere, among many others. It was kind of like the bar, except family friendly.

"Almost there." Jack whispered, his calm expression shifting to a frozen smile.

Skylar wanted to reassure him that the little girl

wouldn't spill everything but thought better of it.

"Okay, here we go." Avery arrived, hefting the cups up onto the table. Pride flushed her face. "Dr. Pepper for Sky and Daddy, Orange Fanta for me."

"Thank you." Sky smiled.

Jack just looked relieved.

After they'd ordered, Avery had taken it upon herself to fill and deliver their beverages of choice.

Jack had opened his mouth and promptly shut it.

Watching the expressions pass over the man's smooth, handsome face had been addicting. Sky had enjoyed the show, although she suspected he was being extra theatrical to gloss over any natural awkwardness they both might feel.

It wasn't a date, per se, but it was definitely a getting to know you type of outing.

The server, a woman in her sixties with a deep drawl and a maternal smile, swooped by to deliver their food and buzzed away with a level of energy Sky found impressive. Mawmaw had had a lot of energy for her age too, but hers had been quiet and contemplative, siphoned into gardening, puzzles, books, and worthwhile discussion. She'd never been one for small talk. A sharp pang echoed in Skylar's chest. *God*, she missed her.

"Daddy said you teach ant-ology." Avery dipped a fry in ketchup, making swirls.

"Anthropology," Jack corrected.

"That's what I said."

Skylar laughed. "Yes, I do."

"My Dad teaches writing and literature. He even writes books."

"Does he?"

"Yeah, but he won't let me read them." The girl rolled her eyes. "He says they're too grown up."

"Not to mention they'd give you nightmares clear

into college," Jack pointed out, taking a bite of his burger.

"Now, I'm intrigued." Skylar nibbled on her own sandwich, but raised her brows at Jack, who just shrugged. She turned her attention back to the girl. "Do you know the titles?"

"Clockwatchers, Frostbitten, Gray Days, and…" She rattled them off, before faltering. Her voice and eyes lowered. "There's another one that he was working on but didn't finish it. That was a while ago."

"Oh?" Sky looked between the two. Jack's animated face had stilled. "I'm sorry. Is everything okay?"

Avery leaned into her father and he threw an arm around her, kissing the top of her head. He looked up with a rueful smile. "I haven't written for a while. I haven't felt the compulsion."

A moment's consideration brought a rush of memory and understanding. *Jack lost his wife, and Avery her mother two years ago.*

She reached across the table and squeezed Jack's arm. "I'm very sorry for both of you."

Jack's gaze met hers. Sorrow seemed endless within his eyes, but cleared just a little as she watched.

"Did you want to see a picture of my mom?" Avery regarded her, her face serious and touched with a child's bewildered grief.

"I would be honored."

The little girl dug in her purse, pulling out a tiny photo album with stuffed bears crowding the shiny cover. She opened it to the first picture and held it up to show Sky.

It was a family photo, Jack looking handsome in a charcoal-colored suit, Avery adorable in a flowered sundress and a pretty dark-haired woman with large, expressive brown eyes and a gentle smile. The photographer had caught them in a lovely candid moment. Both adults gazed at one another with tender affection, while the little girl looked up at them, a broad smile across her tiny face. Avery must have been about four.

"She's quite beautiful."

Avery nodded, putting the little album back in her purse. "She died in a car crash when I was little."

"I'm sorry, sweetie." Sky ached inside for her. "Mine is gone too."

Her eyes widened. "Your Mom died?"

She felt the heavy weight of Jack's stare, but spoke to Avery. "Yes, a very long time ago. My father too."

"You … you're an orphan?" The little girl's lower lip trembled.

"I guess I am, but I had my Mawmaw and she was an awesome grandmother. I also have my big brother who helped look out for me." She smiled in an attempt to ease the tension, hoping to God Avery didn't ask what happened. Past stories and her blank memories weren't something she wanted to discuss with an eight year old. Or anyone, for that matter. "He took his job *very* seriously. It was annoying."

"Did he tell you what to do?"

"Always."

"Did you do what he said?"

"*Never.*"

Avery giggled and Skylar relaxed. She glanced at Jack, relieved to note a smile around his eyes. Without contemplating the gesture, she reached out to and slid her hand into his.

Chapter Fourteen

Stephen woke in the glen. The sun streamed through the woods from the east, casting long, skeletal shadows toward him. He knew immediately where he was, his senses tingling, almost painful in their intensity. Dimly, he wondered whose dream it was. Once upon a time, when Sky was a child, she could pull him into hers. He doubted she even remembered, but it was something he couldn't ever forget.

As he looked around, he contemplated how many times he'd made his way down here to escape either physically, mentally, or both. Dozens? Hundreds? He couldn't even hazard a guess.

He got to his feet, brushing off his jeans, and looked around.

Cognitively, he knew he was in a familiar dreamscape, but the knowledge didn't quell the spike of blood pressure or the surge in his heartrate. The panic in his body pushed back against the struggle for calm in his mind and his muscles trembled.

He hadn't dreamed of this place in a very long time, probably not since he was in his 20's when Sky headed off to college. That time, it had been his, not hers. He could never be completely sure until she made an appearance. If it was her dream, she'd be her current age.

The fort he'd built still nestled within the tree line on the other side of the glen. He'd spent a lot of time constructing it with odd pieces of lumber, stripped branches, tarps, duct tape, and nails. It wasn't too bad for something constructed by an eleven-year-old kid. He'd shown it to Skylar in secret, telling her it was their hiding place during the bad times.

They'd spent too many hours there.

Now, he expected the past to unfold as it had countless times before. Reality hadn't put him in this spot on *that* day, but he knew his imagination wasn't far off. But the ending of the dream always diverted from truth and he'd awaken in a tangled sweaty mess in his own bedroom, gagging on his scream. In his dreams, he hadn't been able to save her.

Squawking from the treetops made his gaze shift upward, as always. Disconcerted, Stephen frowned, his blood shifting in his head with a sudden whoosh.

Three ravens. There had always been one before.

They were just animals. They had no knowledge of the superstitious dread many tribes placed upon them. They did what they did.

Stephen stared up at them and they stared back, seemingly defiant.

They weren't defiant. They were just birds for fuck's sake!

Gooseflesh broke against the surface of his skin when the wind kicked up. It was warm, bringing the metallic scent of an upcoming storm with it. Its warmth couldn't penetrate to dispel the deep chill inside. He could have sworn ice crystals had formed in his blood, turning it to slush. His chest tightened.

The aroma of rain dissipated, replaced by the stink of rotting flesh, oily in his sinuses.

He didn't remember that awful odor in his previous dreams.

Stephen couldn't avert his gaze, nor move away when the figure shoved its way through the woods, turning to the side to traverse the hill downward before climbing up the other side.

Its stench became overwhelming and Stephen gagged.

The figure reached the fort and that's when the

screaming began, high shrieks of pain and terror. From the sound, it was Skylar as a child.

Tears burned his eyes, his horror and the frustration of helplessness merging. His feet rooted, his body remained frozen. Soon, very soon, he should be able to move. He should be able to follow the nightmare to its fruition.

Instead of heading back up the opposite side, as they should have, the two struggling figures came in his direction and stopped a couple yards away.

Stephen still couldn't move. His muscles remained locked as Sky's screams filled the air.

He fought to breathe. The nightmare had changed on him. *This was not how it went.*

The man—no, it wasn't even a man, it was a *thing*. It was little more than a skeleton with rotting meat strung between bones. Cloth hung from its frame in decayed strips. It paused before turning to look at him over its shoulder. The right side of its face was caved into a pulpy mess, the other side charred, one eye melting wetly from its socket. The thing barely looked human. Its voice, filled with heavy phlegm, reached him.

"You're next, you little shit."

Stephen awoke and scrambled upright in bed, gasping. Instead of rot, sour sweat and cigarettes filled his senses.

He turned to look at the clock on his nightstand. 11:13 PM.

Christ, he'd only been asleep an hour.

Something's coming…

Stephen shook his head to dispel the stupid, yet ominous thought.

Three ravens. Why were there three?

Stop it!

He cradled his head in his hands. The urge to call

his sister was persistent, unrelenting.

Stephen looked at the clock again. 11:14 PM.

Sky might very well be up reading. Actually, she likely would be. But what if she'd called it an early night? After all, moving sucked.

Whatever. Fuck it.

With hands shaking more than he would have liked, he grabbed his cell and hit her pre-programmed number. One ring, two, three, four...

When she picked up, a whoosh of stale air left his lungs in relief.

"Hey, Steve. Is something wrong?"

Fear iced her words, but he regretted nothing. He was just glad to hear that she was okay.

"Hey, dork, it's all good. I was just checking in. I figured you might be up reading." Was he speaking too fast? That would make her suspicious.

Sure enough, her voice shifted from fearful to wary. "You never call at this time. Are you really okay?"

"'Course. Just couldn't sleep." He worked to make his tone conversational. "I thought I'd harass my baby sister. How did the move go?"

Sky didn't respond for a few long moments.

He figured she was probably deciding whether to call him on his bullshit or let it pass.

"Yeah, well, it wasn't too bad." She paused and he could sense the sly smile forming and seeping into her voice. Relief flowed through him. He knew she was preparing to push his buttons just because she could. "I had a break and went to lunch with a friend and his adorable daughter."

"His?"

"Yep. Tall, dark, handsome. More than a little yummy."

Stephen winced. "Good thing the kid was with

you."

"Ha ha. And Chloe hasn't slept over at your place *at all* of late?"

"Not tonight." Stephen smiled, the relaxed banter easing his fear.

Just not enough to erase the feeling of foreboding.

Chapter Fifteen

Jack leaned against the doorjamb, watching while Sky spoke with several students. She taught her last class in the main hall, and he'd braved the mass exodus from the stately old building to meet her. She was back in professional mode with her hair up in some kind of complicated braided twist, a collarless sapphire blue top, black skirt, and heels. As gorgeous as she was, he could still admit to himself he preferred her hair loose over her shoulders.

A couple of teenagers started to leave the room, a redheaded boy arching a brow at him as he passed. "Hey, Dr. Langham!"

"Hi, Mike. How's your paper going?"

"It's going. I have other classes, you know." Although defensive sounding, the words held no bite. He was a pretty affable kid.

"Nothing as important as research and writing."

"Oh, I dunno. This class is pretty important too." He glanced over his shoulder at Sky, before grinning at Jack. "A man needs a nice view once in a while."

"Mmhm." Jack somehow doubted Sky wanted anyone taking her classes just to gawk at her. "Yeah, a good instructor can make any material look good."

The kid snorted and hastened out the door, followed by three others before Sky began to gather her materials. She shot him a peripheral glance as he approached. "So, Dr. Langham, I haven't started packing for my escape to Alaska just yet, but I guess it remains to be seen."

"Well, that good to hear. Although, in fairness, it's worth seeing. Amazing scenery, amazing fishing, and I'm fairly certain they have lots of spas and resorts, if that's more your thing." Jack stepped closer and grinned at her.

The morning after their burger run, she'd awakened to a text asking her to dinner or 'if he and Avery had scared her into moving to Alaska.' She'd smiled and texted back that the future was as of yet, undecided.

"How about all of the above?" She snapped her briefcase closed and faced him.

"You fish?" Jack blinked, trying to hold back his surprise and feeling a little bit like a sexist jerk because of it.

"Sure. My brother's almost seven years older than I am. I made it a point to follow him and his best friend around on a regular basis. Drove them both nuts, but I learned a lot." She paused, a tiny frown crinkling between her eyes. "I hunted once or twice too, but that's about it. I could field dress a deer if I really, really had to. Unfortunately, a fair amount of folks I know have to hunt to supplement what's on the dinner table. I didn't need to, so I chose not to."

Jack went blank for a moment before understanding flowed over him. She was an Anthropologist who specialized in Native American studies. Although her skin tone and coloring likely wouldn't be considered exactly traditional American Indian, her almond eyes and sculpted cheekbones heavily hinted at her lineage. "Did you grow up on a reservation?"

"I did. My mother's side is Choctaw."

She didn't offer anything more, so he changed the subject. "Well, providing you're hungry, I have a few possibilities in mind for this evening."

"I'm open. Avery won't be joining us?"

"She's doing the girly sleepover thing with her

BFF, so we actually have the option of going somewhere without a playground or costumed characters."

"I think you underestimate the allure of a swing set, Dr. Langham." She grinned at him and his muscles went a little loose. *What was it about this woman?*

"I'll keep that in mind for next time."

****

Jack chose a steakhouse overlooking the river and guided her through the heavy double doors, his hand barely grazing her back.

They were shown to a table against the large picture window overlooking the rush of the river. In the distance kayakers were practicing rolling while the sun spread orange flames over the water. Hill country pressed on either side, creating the illusion of seclusion within a university town.

The server came by and took their drink orders, and Sky was pleased when Jack made no comment about her non-alcoholic choice. She'd always been amazed how many people would pressure others to drink. She'd been on dates in the past when the guy had actually gotten offended. Those dates hadn't lasted long.

"So, what's the fascination with Alaska?" She looked at him from beneath her lashes without moving her head.

Jack smiled, teeth white against his five o'clock shadow. "My first job out of high school was in the fishing industry up there. Started in the cannery, progressed to the boats. No sleep, but great money."

"My God. Fishing in the Bering Sea? That's insane."

"Yeah, it was, but I was a kid and invincible." He sipped the beer the waiter placed before him. "I lived in Seattle, studying for my undergrad at UW. Every summer I'd work on the boats, save the cash, and live off it during the school year. At the time, it seemed a win-win situation."

"And now?"

"Frankly, I'm amazed I didn't die."

"I'm quite glad of that." She took a sip of her cranberry and Sprite, smiling and nodding when the waiter returned with their meals. "So, you're originally from Washington? No surprise there—you're distinctly lacking any kind of southern drawl. But what brought you to Texas?"

"Ah, the million dollar question. Not a lot of surprises there either. UT scholarship." He sobered, mouth twisting to the side when he stared down at the table.

"You met your wife here." Sky lowered her voice, reached out, and touched his hand.

"I did. Well, Texas, at least. I earned my PhD in Austin, but I taught up in Fort Worth for a time." He leaned forward, steering the topic away from himself. "And, Sky, why are you here? It seems an arbitrary choice. I would have presumed Houston or Austin maybe. Even San Antonio."

Something trembled deep inside her, a little ominous, but she overruled the reaction. "I was born here."

It was Jack's turn to be startled. His brows crept upward. "Really? I didn't think *anyone* was actually from this town. So many folks seem to migrate down here from other parts of the state."

"Surprise! To be honest, I don't really remember it though. I was pretty young."

"Doesn't seem a bad place to raise a kid. Avi loves the children's park. Can't say I blame her. I would too if I were a kid." He sipped his drink, smiling, eyes a little hazed in recollection.

Sky blinked when a large wooden play structure entered the space behind her eyes. *Her mother, beautiful, with dark hair to her waist, pushed her on the swing while the chain creaked. Stephen played football in the field behind and came trotting up to them, grinning but with a tiny trickle of blood running from his lip. He'd announced he'd been the only one to score during the entire game.*

"You okay over there?" Jack pressed her hand. "Fairly certain you were orbiting Venus."

Shaking herself off, she offered him an apologetic smile. "Sorry, just a token memory. Like I said, I don't have many of them."

"How old were you when you moved?"

She didn't answer, spearing a new potato. "Your parents still in Seattle?"

It was a clunky subject change, but her heart had tripped into an instant panicky gallop and she had no clue why. The one memory hadn't been unpleasant.

Jack smoothly followed course and let it drop. "Well, they're in Bellingham. Just a hop away from the border and a little cheaper than Seattle."

"It must be beautiful."

"It is. Avi and I get up there once a year to see them." He chuckled. "And then I'm happy to leave again."

"Ah. Tough relationship?"

"Let's just say I'm too old for a bunch of unsolicited, useless advice regarding myself or my daughter."

"My brother can be like that sometimes. He watched out for me when we were kids. Sometimes he tends to forget I'm thirty now." A laugh popped out. "Every single boyfriend I had was scared of him. I was lucky if I got a handshake at the end of a date."

"I'll have to keep that in mind." His grin quirked to the side, glorifying his dimples.

Her stomach tilted just a little.

Chapter Sixteen

They stepped out into twilight, the early evening caressing with humidity instead of suffocating. A breeze touched her cheek and she turned her face toward it.

"Feel like walking off dinner?" Jack raised his brows, his smile either daring or encouraging her.

"Sure." Sky stepped from her pumps and leaned down to grab them with two fingers. At his dubious expression, she shrugged. "I rarely wear shoes if I can get away with it."

"Any experience with fire ant piles?"

"Unfortunately, yes. Once was all it took though."

He laughed, smoky-blue eyes glinting with good humor as he offered her his arm. "I'm not as bright. It took me a half dozen times, and then I just gave up and always wore shoes."

She slid her hand into the crook of his arm, very conscious of his firm muscles and the faint aroma of aftershave.

They wandered down the sidewalk running parallel to the restaurant and over the footbridge before cutting through the grass toward the river.

Sky slid him a sideways glance, enjoying his profile, prepared to possibly embarrass him. "I read *Clockwatchers*."

He let out a long, agonizing groan and she laughed.

"I enjoyed it. Very imaginative and more than a little creepy. I even picked up the other two, although I haven't had time to start on either one of them just yet."

"Ah, genre fiction. Frowned upon in the academic world but good for a little escapism."

She chuckled. "I'm sure it was fun to write."

"Yeah, it was. Most of them were."

The persistent warm breeze rattled the treetops while late season cicadas played one last desperate song. Nearby traffic had shrunk to the periphery beyond them, the sultry evening pressing close.

"So, how long have you and Avery lived down here?"

"Almost nine months. We lived outside Fort Worth, in Plano. After, well, Nicole died, we hung in for a while, but I just couldn't do it anymore. We needed a change. I got an offer down here, and, well, decided to take it." They stopped and he turned toward her, his face melancholy. "I needed a fresh start."

Sky slid her hand into his, pressing gently. "That must have been rough."

"Yeah, it has been, but I think it was the right choice. Both for Avery and for me." Jack smiled down at her, just a small pull of his lips upward to the side, sadness still touching his voice.

She tilted her chin up to gaze into his eyes. The soft wind tossed around his short waves and without contemplating the move, she reached up to brush her fingers through the hair by his temple. "I'm glad you're both here."

Something changed in his eyes, something she couldn't identify. She lowered her hand and started to pull the other one from his loose grasp. "I'm sorry."

His fingers tightened around hers, firm but gentle. "It's okay. I'm glad we're here too."

They gazed at one another, her heart lurching in her chest. A little light-headed, she managed to pull some air into her stubborn lungs after several long moments. Jack had revealed several facets to his personality—the loving and slightly geeky father, the wounded widower, the charming and funny date, and now this intense and magnetic man. She sensed hesitation in him and understood how torn he must feel.

She didn't recall ever feeling this kind of chemistry before, even with sweet and amiable Casey. Now it seemed like a schoolyard crush. A flicker of guilt drowned itself in a strong wave of want.

Making her choice, she stepped close enough that her breasts skimmed his chest and pushed up on her toes to kiss him, just a delicate brush of her lips to his. After a moment, his mouth softened against hers. It was sweetness, which began to warm under a darkening late summer sky.

His gentle perusal had her melting against him and dropping her shoes. She ghosted her hands up over his arms and shoulders to clasp around his neck. Jack cupped the back of her head in one hand, the other staying at the small of her back to keep her close. Her heart stormed in her ears, reducing her world to his arms.

Sky opened her eyes when he ended the kiss and rested his forehead against hers. "I half expect one or more of our students to happen upon us."

Horror lanced through her and he laughed when she backed away. He caught her hand. "Don't worry. I'm sure they have better things to do."

"I would hope."

Still laughing, he leaned down to grab her shoes. "It's still early. You feel like catching a movie at the Cineplex? Or maybe just taking a drive? We could even head back to my place and watch something R-rated on cable and pop some microwave popcorn without the kiddo lurking in the hallway." He wriggled his brows. "I promise I'll be good."

Skylar laughed with him, instinctively knowing he spoke the truth. He didn't expect anything. Of course, she wasn't so sure about herself. "Sure, but I'd prefer to stop at my place and change. Could I meet you…" She glanced at her watch. "At eight o'clock? Would that be okay?"

"You bet. I'll take you back to your car."

Her hand remained tucked in his.

Chapter Seventeen

Having shed her professional attire in favor of jeans and a boat necked tee, Skylar followed Jack's simple directions to his home. As she drew closer, she slowed her vehicle, her heart beating a little faster than it should.

Was this the same neighborhood?
No, it couldn't be. Could it?

Darkness had settled over the town, so it'd be easy to confuse one neighborhood for another, especially since she was far from familiar with the area. She spotted his address, numbers on display near the porch light. It was the house at the end. She followed the slight curve of the street, parked beside the little craftsman, and stared out at it.

It *was* the same house. Just next door, Sky saw Molly Achen's travel van parked in the driveway in front of her neat little ranch. There was no light coming from the bay windows of her breakfast nook, but a flickering glow from beyond indicated the woman was probably watching television.

Sky returned her gaze to Jack's house, her blood rushing in her ears.

It was as cute and inviting as before. The windows blazed with warmth from within and the man who stirred new feelings in her waited inside.

Still, she hesitated, like some ancient instinct was trying to warn her. It took her another long moment to shake her head and berate herself. *This is stupid. It's just a house, like any other. Wood, cement, drywall, nails, and whatever other materials they use. An inanimate thing.*

"Get a grip," she whispered, climbing from her

SUV and locking it behind her. Pulling in a cleansing breath, she walked up the driveway, crossed to the path leading to the front porch, and rang the bell. Sky summoned a smile.

Jack answered a moment later, his own smile broad. He'd changed into faded jeans and a plain black t-shirt. "Welcome to my humble abode, Dr. Donaghue. Come on in."

He moved to the side and she stepped past him and into the house.

****

Something shifted within the house. Subtle to the naked eye, its ramifications equaled the tossing of a stone into a placid pond, the ripples stretching beyond the point of impact even as the stone tumbled down into the darkness.

Ravens screamed their guttural cries deep from within the forest. Two took flight, landing on the roof of a cute, turquoise colored house. Another joined them an instant later. They tilted their heads, glassy eyes watching.

Molly jerked upright from her recliner, heart lurching in her thin chest when Mr. Chuckles let out a mournful howl. Several dogs in the neighborhood answered him, quieting a few moments later. The night went still again.

Something deep beyond the planks and building materials of a house shifted again, stretched, sighed. And smiled.

****

The front room was cozy, with buffed wooden floors, an overstuffed sectional positioned before a large screen television, a river rock fireplace against the south wall, and a seven-foot bookshelf crammed with volumes, hardbacks, paperbacks, and framed photos. It stood next to a glass slider with impending darkness blanketed against it. A jungle gym stood in the greying light, long shadows stretching behind it. Just beyond, a greenbelt waited on the other side of a short, chain link fence.

Everything is in the wrong place.

Startled, Sky shook her head to dispel the unwarranted thought and shuddered. It was amazingly cold inside. She took a breath, goosebumps marching up and down her arms like soldiers. She shivered and rubbed her arms, the chill pricking her insides.

"Oh, man. Sorry about that!" Jack grimaced and made a beeline for the hallway. His voice floated back at her. "I tend to keep it pretty chilly in here. I guess it's the Seattle in me. Avery and Rosa are always turning it up. It's a continuous battle."

"Rosa?"

He came back, smiling. "My nanny—housekeeper—superwoman. We probably just missed her. I can still smell Windex."

"Ah."

"Have a seat. I was just going to get the popcorn going. Would you like something to drink? We're Dr. Pepper fiends here, but I also have lemonade, iced tea—sorry, not the sweet stuff—I'm not enough of a southerner for that, coffee, and hot chocolate. Thanks to Avery, I even have animal-shaped marshmallows. I can also make up some mock-tails, if you'd like." He stopped and stared at her. "I'm sorry. I'm not babbling, am I?"

"No. No, you're fine. Anything I can help with?" Trying to dismiss the wintry bite sinking into her muscles and bones, she gazed at him, charmed. Apparently, it really had been a long time since he'd dated, let alone invited a woman to his home.

"As of matter of fact, yeah. I have a few movies on the coffee table. Your choice. If none of them appeal,

I can pull some more out." He spoke quickly and Sky tilted her head and raised her brows. He slowed to a stop. "I'm doing it again, aren't I?"

"It's okay." She stepped toward the kitchen. "Let me help and then we'll both choose tonight's entertainment. Maybe we could make some hot chocolate, if you're good with that."

The little door next to fridge leads to the attic. Tall people can't stand up there.

Skylar frowned.

"Everything okay?" Jack paused, hanging on the refrigerator door.

"Sure, of course. Now, what can I do?"

Ten minutes later, she sank into Jack's deep sofa, their spread of snacks and drinks on the coffee table before them. He popped the movie in, adjusted his settings and lowered himself next to her, close but not touching. Frowning, he turned to study her. "Are you still cold? I can feel it from here."

Sky had been attempting to control her body from trembling and her teeth from chattering, a little unnerved. It felt like it was forty degrees in his house, but she could see a slight sheen to Jack's brow. "A little."

Jack grabbed a blanket from the back of the couch and flipped it open to cover her. He seemed to hesitate just a moment before scooting closer and draping his arm around her. On instinct, she nestled into him, sighing against the warmth and scent of him.

"Better?" He leaned down and kissed her, just a soft brush and smile behind it.

"Mmhm." A little.

"Showtime." He hit play and they settled in to watch a classic noir they'd both decided on.

****

Jack felt heavy shudders pulse through Sky's

105

small frame, a deep chill rising from her. His temperature naturally ran on the higher side, but it did nothing to warm her despite his embrace. Half way through the film, she looked up at him, face apologetic.

"I'm sorry, Jack, but I think I must be overtired or something. It might be best if I called it a night."

"I hope you're not getting sick." He clicked off the movie, rose, and pulled her to his feet. Touching her cheek, he was surprised when her skin remained icy under his palm. "God, you're still so cold."

She nodded, jaw quivering. "I think I'm going to go home, hide under an avalanche of blankets, and sleep it off."

"Hold up a moment." Jack crossed the entry, pulling open the closet cattycorner to the front door. He pulled a sweatshirt off a hanger and brought it over, draping it over her shivering body. "I know it'll be huge on you, but take it home anyway. I'll collect it from you next time."

"Thank you." She slid her arms into the sleeves, pushing them up so at least her hands were visible. Reaching over, she grabbed her handbag off the end of the couch. "I'm so sorry, Jack. I'm not sure what's going on. I felt fine before."

"It's okay. It happens." He put his arm around her shoulders and they walked to the front door. He kissed her temple, satisfied to see a tiny smile stretch her lips in response. "I'll walk you to your car. You okay to drive?"

"I'll be fine."

They stepped out onto the porch and Jack followed as Sky walked down the driveway.

****

The woods cast long shadows from the east as the sun crept up over the horizon. The early morning should have encouraged all manner of critters to pursue breakfast before the heat of the day sent them into hiding.

But Sky didn't hear anything beyond the occasional snap of a twig under her own feet. The glen and surrounding woods remained still, as if holding a collective breath to wait for something beyond her comprehension.

The area shouldn't have been familiar, but a distant part of her recognized her own stubborn refusal. She'd been here before but couldn't begin to figure where "here" was, let along the when or why behind it.

She wandered, kicking small stones, careful not to trip in undergrowth before opting to follow the perimeter. The woods were dense, as if pressing together to prevent her passage. She didn't see any paths leading into the forest, at least nothing wide enough to allow any creatures larger than a squirrel. Fear iced her veins, accelerating her heartrate.

She carefully descended into the glen and up the other side. On the northeast edge, she came across a child's fort hidden within the trees. It was more a crude lean-to than anything, assembled with branches and cast-off pieces of lumber. A camouflage tarp covered the would-be roof in an attempt to weatherproof, attached with nails and duct tape. Sky dropped into a crouch to peer inside.

Another tarp served as flooring, covered with a couple of ratty blankets, one dark blue with stars, the other deep purple with yellow and white butterflies. Dread crept through her, thick and pervasive. Without pulling it out, she knew there'd be red-brown droplets stained into the wings of one butterfly. Swallowing nausea, she swept her gaze over several stuffed animals, books, and a few action figures. A dusty battery-powered lantern stood in one corner. She flinched when it automatically switched on to illuminate several colored photos of mountains, glacial waters, spiring evergreens, bears, and eagles. They'd been haphazardly cut from magazines and attached to the interior wall with more duct tape.

Rocking back on her heels, acidic bile rose in her throat and she fought the inclination to be sick.

She wouldn't remember. She *refused* to.

Droplets of sweat broke through her flesh, running into her eyes, sticking her blouse to her back. She swiped her forehead with the heel of her hand, muscles taut and trembling.

The beating of heavy wings broke the silence and she glanced up just in time to see the raven land in one tree far above her. It cocked its head, as if to get a better look at her.

"What do you want?" Her voice shook and disgust rose within when she recognized her panic. A deep chill oozed into her bones, setting her teeth to chatter. "Am I destined to die early? Is that it?"

It fluffed its feathers and cawed, its voice bouncing around the still woods.

Her own breath rasped in her ears, escalating to a hoarse scream when something grabbed her by the upper arm and dragged her from the fort and into the woods.

****

Skylar almost brought the scream with her into the waking world, but it stuck inside, strangling her, the sound shrinking to a harsh gasp. Heart pounding, she blinked hard once, twice. Her head felt thick, fuzzy, as she peered around the darkened bedroom to verify she was alone.

It had been years since she'd had that dream. Despite knowing she was safe, her muscles continued to quake and an intense headache throbbed above and behind her eyes. Her body dripped with sweat and swallowing felt like she'd gargled with shards of glass.

Shit. Maybe she really *was* sick.

Swinging her feet off the side of the bed, she pushed herself to stand, pausing to ride out a wave of dizziness. Stumbling from her bedroom, she used the wall for support as she made her way to the bathroom, searching for a thermometer.

A temperature of 102.7 stared back at her.

With shaking hands, she washed some acetaminophen down with cool water and went back to bed.

Chapter Eighteen

Chloe had stopped by the garage to let him know her evening would be spent with her books preparing for some big test. She'd called him a "distraction," giving him a hard but all too brief kiss before swaying off. He always enjoyed watching her hips sway. She'd glanced over her shoulder, smirking when she caught him looking. He smirked back.

And then there was the fact that the poker brigade wouldn't land at his place until tomorrow night, bringing all their extra smoke, swearing, and flatulence. It was also always BYOB when Stephen played host. The guys were all aware of how he rolled.

So, now Stephen steeled himself. After months of avoiding them, he figured it was time to sift through his grandmother's boxes. Right after Mawmaw passed, he'd selfishly thought Skylar should have been the one to do it. After all, didn't women usually do that stuff? He'd hinted and she'd ignored. Knowing their grandmother had never been a packrat, they both feared what they might find. Then Sky up and moved away, knocking the responsibility back into his court.

Well, hell.

Maybe it was because of the nightmare. He hadn't had it in so long and now it had shifted enough to freak him out even more than he remembered. Its vibrations still flowed over him during that soft time just before sleep took him. He'd often say a silent prayer he wouldn't be tortured by the damned dream again.

With a sudden burst of breath, he grabbed both boxes and placed them on his kitchen table. Pulling out his pocket knife, he careful split the tape on the smaller box and pulled back the flaps.

Relief siphoned clear to his toes. It was filled with school papers, projects, report cards, birthday cards, and pictures. He piled them outside the box, grinning as he recognized work clear back to his middle school years, not long after they'd arrived in Durant. He'd never thought of Mawmaw as sentimental and some part of him was ecstatic to be wrong. This box proved that he'd had happiness in his childhood. Sometimes he forgot.

He cut open the other one, finding similar artifacts from Skylar's childhood. Of course, there was much more. Stephen found one of her report cards from first grade, his smile slipping when he read several teacher comments. Words like "fearful," "shy," and "uncommunicative" were common. As she grew, teacher notes morphed more to words like "intelligent," "bright," "curious," and one said "relentless." He chuckled as he continued to poke through the box, finding childish drawings and typed reports. If he made his way south, he'd have to bring the box with him. They'd probably laugh over all the dread they'd silently amassed over these mystery boxes.

Then he hesitated.

A large manila envelope tucked at the very bottom of the box made him raise his eyebrows, before pulling them together in a frown.

Across the front "My Dearest Grandchildren" was written in Mawmaw's neat and compact cursive.

His hands shook as he ripped it open and dumped the contents. Thick rubber-banded bundles of envelopes fell onto the table and his breathing hastened, becoming uncomfortable, drying his throat. He opened the first one, reading a letter from Mawmaw addressed to both he and Sky, stomach tightening. He took note of several official looking envelopes, then pushed them aside. The others were addressed to Mawmaw and had been opened carefully. Stephen could picture her sitting at her desk, slicing them with that little letter opener with sunflowers embossed on it.

Nausea rippled through his belly when he unfolded the first one and began reading. Three letters later, he threw up his late lunch.

Maybe it really had been Pandora's Box.

****

Benny guided the steering wheel of his old Bronco with two fingers, singing along with the Pointer Sisters in a cracking falsetto. He passed his usual turn, taking the main road farther out, where properties widened just a smidge. His parents, sister, brother, nephews, nieces, aunts, uncle, seven cousins, grandfather, and hundred and six year old great-grandmother lived out this way, but so did Steve.

On the seat next to Benny lay Stephen's wallet. He'd found it by the lockers and figured his friend might be flipping out just about now. He could have called, sure, but Benny's gut said he should just bring it by. Steve had been wired tight since Skylar left, and Ben could admit he was worried. For Steve and his 'lil sis.

He made a right at the Kwik Chek, a left past the barbeque place, went straight for a mile and a half, and then made another right. Pulling to the curb just past Steve's Silverado, he grabbed the wallet and hopped out, making long strides to the front door. Benny knocked once before letting himself in. Steve didn't lock the door, unless he was gone or asleep.

"Yo, Steve!"

As usual, the place smelled like cigarettes and Pine Sol. Stevie Ray Vaughn strummed from the stereo, volume low. Benny didn't hear anything else.

He passed the eat-in kitchen, noting a couple of boxes on the table top with dumped contents across the veneer, but didn't offer them another glance. "Steve?"

A light glowed off the hallway, but his friend didn't answer. Dread crept into his belly, freezing him from the inside out. Benny's steps slowed, but he forced himself forward.

The bathroom was the first door on the right, and light spilled from within. Bracing himself, his body sweating with tension, he looked inside. And promptly released his breath is a whoosh.

"Damn, Steve. You scared the shit outta me!" He smiled because he was more prone to that than a scowl.

Stephen sat on the linoleum, wedged between the tub and the toilet. He looked up, face ashen, and Benny's smile froze for an agonizing second before dropping away. "Steve, what happened?"

Deeply shadowed, the man's gaze latched onto his. "I don't know what to do, man."

Benny crouched down, softened his voice. "About what? Is Sky okay?"

"Um, yeah. I think so. I *hope* so. I haven't spoken to her lately." He smiled, but there was nothing pleasant in it. "I never knew what happened after we left *that* night. Not really. Mawmaw told us, well, me, a few things, but it wasn't the truth. She didn't tell me the *truth*."

"I'm sure she had her reasons. Your grandmother was a great woman. She wouldn't have ever done anything to hurt you or Sky."

"No, no. Of course not." Stephen shook his head, his voice barely a whisper. He slapped a hand to his chest. "She was protecting me."

"That sounds just like your Mawmaw."

"I should have questioned more, man. I should have, I don't know, sensed something was off in the story she told me."

Benny had no idea what he was talking about. Rumors he'd heard over the years didn't replace truth. They probably didn't even come close. "You were a kid, Steve. Whatever happened scarred you, traumatized you. By blocking it, Skylar probably got the better deal."

"I can't stand the thought of Sky, or anyone else, hating me. Especially my baby sister." Stephen's eyes took on a weary, haunted look, aging him before Benny's eyes.

"She could never hate you."

The man just shook his head, mumbling something Benny couldn't quite hear. It sounded like, "I wouldn't blame her."

"Come on, man. Let's get you off the floor and outta the can. Not to sound like an old lady or anything, but I'm gonna make us some coffee, tea, or something, and you're going to tell me what the hell is going on. Whatever you finally decide to spill to me will not change the fact that you are and will always be my best friend. Got it?"

Stephen stared at him for a full minute before nodding. He pushed himself up and Benny grabbed his arm to help him the rest of the way.

Chapter Nineteen

Avery Langham peered through the chain link separating her backyard from the dense woods beyond it. The fence wasn't all that tall, just eye level with her. It would be easy enough to climb over and follow that little path if she chose to.

The rain had finally stopped, leaving the air humid and sticky. Sun peeped through the clouds, sending out some intense rays despite the few orange and yellow leaves signaling the end of summer. Her Dad said Texas weather was capricious. Avery looked the word up once and had to agree with him.

"So, what do you think? Wanna go?" Bailey, Avery's very best friend, smiled, showing off two missing teeth. Her freckles and large glasses fought for dominance on her small face. "We could be explorers."

"I'm not sure." Although the slow cooker had already been set, Rosa would bustle around the house cleaning real and imagined dust from everything, waiting until Dad got home before leaving for the night. Avery wondered if the old lady would notice if she slipped out of the yard just for a few minutes.

"My brother said it's not far, but the path gets kinda narrow. Okay for us, but tight for older kids and grownups."

Avery glanced over her shoulder past the jungle gym and through the sliding glass door into the living room. At that moment, she heard a fury of water running in the utility room sink. *Ah ha.* Rosa was getting ready to mop the kitchen and bathrooms. She tended to shoo Avery out of the house or, at least to her bedroom, when she mopped and it always took *forever*.

Now or never.

"Okay." She shoved one sneaker-clad foot into a diamond-shaped opening in the chain link and then another, before pulling herself up and over. Bailey scrambled behind her and they both stared at the uneven path cutting a thin slice through the woods.

Although Bailey had been the one to suggest the exploration, Avery set out first, her friend following close behind. As soon as she stepped under the canopy, the temperature dropped several degrees, but she continued forward, enjoying the contrast of the sudden chill.

The forest seemed to curl around them, almost as if they were being swallowed, and Avery pushed back the disturbing thought. Birds called from the treetops and she glanced up just in time to see black wings against a speck of blue sky before it disappeared into the foliage. Undergrowth rustled as small critters ran along the forest floor and Avery paused, considering the possibility of snakes.

"Is something wrong?" Baily asked from a posted position of less than an inch behind her.

"No." Avery was fairly certain snakes would be going into hibernation about now. Besides, Dad once said most critters were more afraid of people and would stay away from them if at all possible. Taking note of that memory, she stepped heavier and harder, trying to make more noise. Just in case.

The thick trunk of a tree angled across the path and although they were able to walk beneath without issue, she figured most adults would have to crouch or crawl. Somehow this knowledge made the hike feel even more like an adventure, like it was only for kids, kind of like in the movies or even in some books she'd read.

Just before them, the woods grew a little lighter as they approached the end of the path. She stepped out into the clearing, blinking a little in the late afternoon sun. Several feet beyond, the land sloped down into what looked like a mini canyon. Avery inched closer, relieved to see it wasn't particularly deep, but from side to side, it was wide. Maybe they could walk around it, but there was no way to say how far a walk it would be. If they were careful, they could clamber down to the bottom and up the other side in no time at all.

"What do you think?" Bailey appeared next to her, squinting down the hill. "There's a little bit of water running down there. It's just a little stream. Maybe we could jump it."

"Maybe." Avery stared down into the glen, studying the foliage and slow current of what she hoped was shallow water. "Wait. Look!" She pointed.

"What?" Bailey raised a hand to blot out the sun.

"There's a bridge down there. Well, kinda. It's a little hidden in some long grass, but it looks kind of like the balance beam at school. It goes right across the water."

"Oh! I see it!"

Without waiting, Avery scurried sideways fifteen feet down the embankment, careful to watch where she put her feet. She crossed to the makeshift bridge, pushing against it with the toe of her sneaker. It seemed pretty solid. Holding her arms straight out, she walked across it, turning to check on her friend when she hit the other side.

Bailey was right behind her.

They climbed up the next slope, turning it into a race, both giggling and breathing hard when they reached the top. Avery looked around. It didn't look that different than the other side.

"So, there's some kind of treehouse over here? I hope it's not one of those deer spotting places." Avery scrunched her face.

"I dunno. I don't *think* so…" Bailey frowned in thought.

Loud caws from above had both girls tilting their heads back. Two big black birds hopped around on a branch above them, looking down. They cawed again, louder, more insistent.

"Oh man, they're gonna poop on us." Bailey edged sideways. "I think we invaded their territory."

"Maybe." Avery no longer watched the birds. She'd spotted what must be the "treehouse" Bailey's brother spoke of. "I think your brother needs to look up the definition of *treehouse*."

"Huh?"

About fifteen yards east of them, a pile of sticks resembling some kind of shelter melted into the tree line. Curious, Avery edged closer. It looked like a lean-to somebody had built a long time ago. Maybe even a fort. She saw the glint of what once was silver duct tape. It looked like it was rotting.

She jumped when Bailey grabbed her arm and pulled her back. "I don't think this is a good idea."

"Why? I was just going to peek inside." Avery frowned at her. "You're being goofy."

"What if someone lives in there?" Bailey still held onto her arm, her fingers digging in.

"Why would somebody live in there?" Avery considered for a moment. "They'd have to be really short."

"The smaller the shelter, the warmer it would be for them."

"How would you know that?" Avery straightened and peered at her friend, curious.

"My oldest brother said he knew someone who lived in their car for a while. He said the guy just filled it with newspapers and other junk, saying it was warmer. Like insulation."

"Oh." She cast another look at the little fort thing, wondering if it wouldn't be a neat idea to set up a tent out here as a secret place just for her. Despite what Bailey said, the lean-to thing didn't look big enough for an adult. Avery suspected it had been built a very long time ago by kids. They may have had the right idea.

"Anyway, it looks creepy." Bailey rolled her eyes. "And you're right, Tyler doesn't have a *clue* what a treehouse is."

"And he thinks he's so smart." Bailey's brother was twelve and Avery didn't consider him particularly intelligent. He just liked to pretend he knew more because he was in middle school.

"Well, *we* know he's a dummy."

Both girls giggled. Since Avery didn't have any brothers or sisters, she was happy to assist in making fun of any friend's siblings.

"Wanna go back and climb on the monkey bars?" Bailey turned to head back the way they'd come.

"Okay." Avery started to follow, but paused. For just a split second, she thought she caught the scent of something burning. It wasn't barbeque either. A Texas girl knew that scent. This was something strong and unpleasant.

It passed almost as soon as she noticed it. Shaking her head, she forgot about it when she hurried to catch up with her friend.

Chapter Twenty

Stephen watched his best friend make coffee and bring two large mugs to the kitchen table. He nodded his thanks when Benny set his on the placemat before him.

Most of the contents of both boxes had been replaced, except for a couple personal letters and official ones. They sat just to his left. His eyes would wander toward them before snapping forward. Maybe part of him expected them to disappear.

It was after ten and Stephen had told Benny everything. Wasn't he supposed to feel better? Wasn't spilling your guts supposed to result in profound relief, a lightening of the soul or whatever? He didn't feel any of that. He just felt weary beyond the bone. Fear from earlier hadn't abated.

Benny had said little, but had listened with an intensity indicative of his character. He'd nodded, shaken his head, even grunted in acknowledgement here and there. He didn't seem to judge, just absorb. Very soon he would voice his thoughts. That's how he'd always been: listen, absorb, ponder and then, he'd give his honest opinion. He was still in the pondering part of the process. Stephen couldn't say how long it would take.

The ticking of the clock above the kitchen doorway competed with the low melancholy croon of Elliott Smith from the stereo in the living room. Stephen took a sip of his coffee, figuring Benny probably found the decaf he'd bought on a lark when he considered cutting back his caffeine. That purchase had been a mistake.

Benny folded his arms on the table and cleared his throat.

Miserable, Stephen eyed him, waiting.

"That's a lot of shit to carry on your shoulders, Steve." Benny pulled in a deep breath. "But I can see why, man. I mean, how could you *not* feel guilty, considering everything? But you were a *kid*. You were fucking twelve years old."

Stephen said nothing. He didn't remember ever feeling like a kid.

"I guess I'm looking at it this way—you made a choice. I get that, but, like I said, you were a little kid. But your mother also made a choice and I have no doubt she knew the ramifications of that choice. She did what any mother would have done. I can tell you, my own mom would have made the same choice in a heartbeat. That's what they do."

"But, how can I even tell Sky?"

"You're her big brother, man. She loves you." Stephen opened her mouth to speak and Benny waved him off. "I'm not saying it isn't going to be rough. I know she can be ... difficult, but your relationship is strong enough to survive it. Besides, it's not just your story to tell. At least, not anymore. I hope you realize that."

"I don't know. It's my fault she doesn't even remember our mother."

"It's because of *you* that your sister is *alive* today." Benny shook his head and his low voice rumbled with a touch of rare anger. "Besides, it all happened a lifetime ago. No one can change *any* of it, and you damn well know you have a second chance here. It'll definitely be hard, probably awkward and weird too, but you have an opportunity not many people get."

Stephen stared at his friend for a full minute, who gazed back with his brows lifted, nonplussed. He finally broke contact, nodding. "I guess I have some phone calls to make. I'm not even sure she'll see me. In her letter,

Mawmaw said she didn't want us to know."

"She'll see you." Benny's voice left no room for question. "And once you arrange something, I'd be happy to tag along, I mean, if you want some support. It's been a while since I've gone on a road trip."

"Thanks, Ben. I'd appreciate that."

"No problem." Benny's tone drifted into uncertainty a moment later. "Have you thought when you're going to tell Skylar?"

The horror of it slid into Stephen yet again and he felt cold. "I think I … um … man, I'm not sure. I'll want to drive down and tell her in person." He tried to smile. "She can't hit me if I'm not there."

"That's quite considerate of you."

"I do my best." He tried on a strained smile.

Benny chuckled, rose, and smacked him on the shoulder.

Chapter Twenty-One

Sky called in sick Monday morning. The fever had broken the previous night, but she'd felt too weak and shaky to teach her classes. By three, the fog lifted and she chalked it up to some forty-eight-hour bug. She was just thankful it wasn't the flu.

Now, restless, she busied herself with unpacking—unwrapping dinnerware, kitchen tools, utensils, framed photos, dust collectors, and a variety of other possessions she didn't remember owning. She found spots for décor, changed it around, and then put them back again. Books were alphabetized and shelved on her fiction and non-fiction floor to ceiling maple shelving. She dragged the stepladder from one end of the house to the other, positioning wall hangings, stepping back, staring and straightening, using a leveler if need be.

Her mind, no longer filled with mud, had returned to the nightmare and she hoped to dispel it in housework. It hadn't haunted her in almost twenty years. Why now? What if its reprisal was indicative of that deep, dark secret pushing to get out now?

The mere thought of that psychological barrier crumbling scared the hell out of her, but at the same time, she wondered if it might be time.

As much as she tried not to ruminate on it, her odd reaction to Jack's home bothered her. In the few moments between leaving the house and getting into her car, she'd been warm again. She was positive about that. The cold had snapped back and tepid air had rushed in to enfold her.

And then there was the instinctive knowledge she'd been in that house before. She wanted, in fact, she *needed* to think it was a childhood playmate's house.

The inner lie reverberated. Part of her considered talking to Stephen, but she didn't want to contemplate his reaction. Or overreaction.

The fireplace was wrong. It hadn't been river rock. It had been worn brick.

If nothing else, the prospect of going back into that house made her uneasy, at best. But how in the world could she bring something like *that* up to Jack? He'd think she'd popped her top.

Taking a break, she shoved unwanted suppositions away. Pouring herself some strawberry lemonade, she pushed through the screen door slider and onto her little covered back patio. She dropped into her cushioned wicker loveseat and stretched her legs onto the matching ottoman, crossing her ankles.

Texas had a unique tendency of dropping a full day's rain within a ten to fifteen minute window. It would blur the world as it pounded the rooftop of the house and the awning above her, the noise deafening, but somehow cleansing. Just down the gentle slope from the back of her property, the river would rise, twisting and churning with whitewater, the complete antithesis to the placid current that propelled many an inner tuber downstream during a pristine summer day.

She enjoyed the late afternoon show, gasping in delight when lightening touched hill country from one end to the other, filling the overcast sky with a show of electrical threads that somehow seemed alive.

The intensity of the shower lessened the moment her doorbell rang.

Sky considered ignoring it but curiosity nixed the impulse.

She slipped back inside and crossed to the door to find Jack standing on her front step. A touch of a smile pulling to one side made her stomach flutter just a little.

He held up a paper bag. "I feel kind of responsible for you not feeling well, so I brought Rosa's chicken and rice soup. Legend has that this stuff performs miracles."

"Hi, Jack. Thank you." Sky gazed up at him, the tiny war inside waning and extinguishing before it barely began. She moved aside to let him in.

Hesitating, he tilted his head. "My first thought is I don't want to enter the sick house. No offense. The next one thinks that you're looking much better than you did on Friday."

"I feel better. It was a crappy weekend, but it seemed to lift a few hours ago. Just a malicious, but mercifully short bug. I was out back enjoying the storm. You could join me, if you'd like." Sky said the words, meaning them, wondering how bad of an idea it was. "I have strawberry lemonade."

Jack stared at her for a few moments longer, shrugged, and stepped inside. "Real men don't say no to strawberry lemonade."

She laughed. It felt good. The last time she'd laughed, she'd been in his company. She remembered how sweet he'd been, adjusting the thermostat, despite his own discomfort, tucking a blanket around her, pulling her into his side to keep her warm, all the while keeping his hands from roaming.

"Wow. You've been busy." Jack looked around. "Looks cozy and lived in."

"Yeah, having towers of boxes gets old and..." She shrugged. "I was restless."

"I understand. I stopped by home briefly for soup and left just as Rosa started vacuuming my drapes. Seriously. She was *vacuuming* my drapes."

Skylar laughed. "Where's Avery?"

"Her friend's mom picked them up after school for a birthday party at Chuck E. Cheese. One of their classmates apparently reached the big nine."

"I see. It's an important age."

"Most definitely."

"C'mon." She took his arm. "Strawberry lemonade, remember? I made it myself, if you count putting frozen glop in a pitcher and adding 3 ½ cans of water."

This time he laughed and waited while she stuck his offered soup in the fridge and pulled out a pitcher to pour him a glass and refresh her own. He then followed her out to the back patio. They sat together, close in the love seat, and watched the weather unfold before them, quiet while the rain thundered against the awning above them.

"Been in Texas over a decade and the storms still continue to amaze me." He turned to her with a grin, meeting her eyes.

Sky should have looked away, across her backyard, down toward the torrent of river, maybe commenting how she hoped it didn't rise too much or something equally inane. She didn't.

As she gazed at him, she soaked in details, just little ones. A sprinkling of early silver at his temple, a day's growth of dark beard on his cheek and jaw, a tiny scar at his hairline, eyes a fusion of smoke and blue. She thought about his relationship with his daughter, how the little girl adored him and vice versa. She remembered the pain in his eyes when he spoke of his late wife, his admitted reluctance to move on. He'd managed to take a small first step. With her.

It's just a house. Brick, mortar, whatever. It's just a house.

Despite everything, she wouldn't backslide. She didn't quite remember when he'd become so important.

"Sky?" Her name was just a breath on his lips, so

close to hers. His eyes deepened with want.

She didn't retreat and his mouth moved warm and soft against hers. She touched his face with her fingertips and his arm went around her, his hand against the small of her back. He tasted of cinnamon and coffee when he deepened the kiss.

After a few lovely moments, they parted and he smiled into her eyes. "I think you just gave me your cooties."

"My apologies." She giggled, unable to help herself.

Thunder shook the heavens as Sky leaned her head against his shoulder and closed her eyes, wondering what it would be like to sleep with him. She could count her lovers on one hand, in part, thanks to her brother's scary demeanor, but she could also thank her own ambition. It hadn't allowed for much of a social life.

Her thoughts fell to the just-in-case box of condoms in her nightstand drawer and wondered when her libido in stasis had started to reawaken. Knowing the answer, she opened her eyes and gazed up at Jack's profile. It was a good profile, attractive without veering into pretty boy. How did he manage to be rugged, yet elegant? Both descriptions seemed incongruous, but yet, here he was.

As if sensing her scrutiny, he pulled his gaze from the storm and met hers. Her breath hitched when his eyes darkened and his expression shifted, but he swallowed and looked away, as if beating down some part of himself. Hunger she'd glimpsed a few moments ago had returned, seemingly sharpening his discomfort.

It occurred to her he was the type of man who would remain true to his wife's memory, unable to compromise himself or her with the physicality of simple sex. He'd want more. She wasn't sure if she *could* give him more.

A yearning inside strove to drive away the superstitions and concentrate on her own emotions and the reality of what her five senses told her. Allowing her mind to shake away her worries, she rose before she could second guess herself and held out her hand.

He gazed up at her, expression sliding between surprise, uncertainty, and indecision.

Saying nothing, she waited, wondering if it would hurt as much as she thought it might if he were to say no. What an odd position to be in. In the past, all she'd had to do was crook a little finger and the man in her life would fall all over himself.

Jack stood, towering above her. When she wore heels, the height difference didn't feel quite as dramatic. Or maybe she was just deluding herself.

"Are you sure?" His voice sounded raspy in hesitation.

"Mmhm." Sky took his hand and led him through her tiny living room and down the hall to the master bedroom at the end.

Reaching up, she pressed her hands to either side of his face, looking into his blue-gray eyes, watching his residual indecision disappear.

He leaned down, brushing her mouth with his once, twice, before pressing in.

Her heart whooshed in her ears, excitement and more than a little fear settling over her. She knew she was in danger of losing her heart to this man, but couldn't seem to stop it. The momentum had already begun. She parted her lips for him and he accepted the invitation, flicking his tongue just inside for a quick taste or tease before sliding it against hers.

Without losing the connection, she dropped her hands to his chest, quickly undoing the buttons of his shirt, happy to find bare warmth beneath. His flesh was smooth, hairless, muscles lean and solid. She shoved the garment off his shoulders and he shifted to let it fall to the floor, before wrapping his arms around her waist.

He slid his fingers just under her sweatshirt, his touch eliciting tingles of pleasure across her midsection.

Sky broke away and stepped back, enjoying the blatant desire etched into his face. In one fluid movement, she tugged her top up and over, letting it drop as well. She hadn't bothered with a bra that morning and his eyes widened.

He swallowed. "You're gorgeous."

Smiling at him when he closed the gap, she pulled in a quick breath when his hands smoothed over her, thumbs brushing her nipples. When he replaced his hands with his mouth, she sunk her fingers in his thick hair, her head falling back, eyes closing. His caresses sent tiny electrical currents through her and a flare of heat burst low in her belly.

****

Straightening, Jack gazed into those amazing violet-blue eyes as they darkened. Goosebumps swept across her creamy flesh, while her chest heaved and her body trembled. He swept her up into his arms and they tumbled onto the bed, hands smoothing, exploring, fingers curling.

Hooking his fingers in her waistband, he peeled her leggings and panties down and off, gazing at her long smooth legs and the dark blonde juncture. Some distant clanging touched base with what little logic he possessed not eclipsed by his lizard brain. "I don't have any protection."

Without a word, she nodded toward her nightstand. He reached over and clumsily reached to pull one square packet out and dropped it next to them.

He crawled over her, leaning in to touch his lips to her forehead, nose, cheeks, spending time nuzzling her throat, lightly rubbing his beard growth against her skin. He moved down her body, planting warm, wet kisses as he went. He was so hard he ached, but he could wait, enjoying the sound of her low gasp and the effect he had on her.

Jack made love to her with his tongue and lips, taking his time and savoring her responses. Several moments later, she arched, a soft cry escaping her lips and he smiled against her.

He moved back up her body, trailing kisses over her flushed skin before hovering over her. He gazed into her beautiful eyes as she blinked away the blindness of her climax.

"I've wanted you since I saw you at the park." He whispered, sincere. He almost mentioned noting the color of her bra strap that day—lavender—but decided against it. A writer's observations could easily slide into perceived creepiness.

"Did you?" Her voice was no more than a breath.

"Mmhm … all sweaty and sexy. How could I not?" He smirked when she unfastened his fly, sucking in a breath when she reached inside with a gentle hand. Maneuvering his hips, he quickly disposed of his jeans before gazing down at her, elbows locked. She slid the condom on, looking at him through her lashes.

"So…" Her brows crept up and a soft smile curved her full lips. "Sweaty and sexy?"

"God, yes." He kissed her throat, gently sucking her pulse point, careful not to leave a mark. "Damned sexy, sweaty, not sweaty, dressed for work, or just wearing a denim shirt with a dust smudge on your right cheek. Or naked. Definitely while naked."

"You're not so bad yourself." Sky chuckled,

enfolding her arms around him to pull him against her and then into her. He paused, but at her shaky nod, they glided together, his worries and fears dissipating in a haze of desire and affection. He saw only Skylar. Her golden hair spread across the pillow, her mouth parted slightly, eyes dipping. She was so damned beautiful.

Their gentle rocking hastened as they clung together, fingers threading, palms pressing. Covered in sweat, their breathing became harsher, kisses deeper, wetter, their bodies meeting with more force.

When she constricted around him, he watched her eyes close and head tip back. Another cry escaped her lips, but low and throaty. Jack followed a moment later, burying his face in her hair and kissing the lobe of her ear. Heart thrumming, trembling just a little, he maneuvered to the side and gathered her to him. He pressed his lips to her temple, pleased to see a sleepy smile curve her mouth.

A few moments later, her breathing deepened. He watched her sleep, feeling content for the first time in too long. A moment later, he followed her into a relaxed slumber.

Chapter Twenty-Two

Sky stood on the path, just a few yards from the clearing and the glen. Twilight hung heavy and expectant, the air still and squeezing around her. Across the chasm, a light burned in the fort, a small shadow shifting within.

Breath wheezing in her ears, she walked forward, careful where she stepped, vigilance enmeshed with adulthood. At one time, the path was so familiar, her movements took little to no thought.

She emerged from the trees, the ghost of the moon low in the sky, casting a white glow to gray her surroundings. Above, as if they'd been expecting her, the ravens cawed, hopping from branch to branch, taking flight in a flurry and blur of dark feathers.

Just behind her, she heard the snapping of branches and the shuffling of large feet. Slurred oaths rumbled from down the path and Sky glanced around, unsure which direction to go. This was a different take on the dream. She'd never been the observer before.

"Sky?"

She turned toward her name, the voice soft but recognizable. Uncertainty soaked into the single syllable of the word.

Jack stood in the clearing just north of her. He wore the same button up and khakis he'd worn to her home. Face in shadows, he tilted his head toward her and held out his hand.

Behind her, the sound of something large shoved its way in her direction, moving faster than ever before. Pivoting, she darted toward Jack, just as the thing burst from the woods. She didn't have time to evade, heart shuddering as she expected the blow, gasping when ice-

*water splashed over her and the father-thing from her
imagination staggered right through her.*

*Her own breath plumed around her as she stared
after it, muscles locking and shaking.*

*"What the hell is that?" Jack appeared next to
her, glancing between her and her nightmare.*

*It stumbled down the embankment and up the
other side, leaning forward to keep balance.*

*"No." Sky hadn't realized she'd whispered the
word, her world frozen around her as the monster
reached the fort.*

Skylar whipped her eyes open, a cry stuck deep in
her throat. After a long moment of disorientation, she
remembered where she was, her cheek against Jack's
warm chest, swelling and falling with the gentle rhythm
of his steady breaths. When she looked up at him, she
found him staring back, fleeting puzzlement touching his
brow before smoothing.

"You okay?"

She didn't find her voice right away, giving him a
smile she expected was far from reassuring. "Mmhm."

Jack tightened his arms around her, pressing a
tender kiss to brow. "You sure?"

"Of course." Wanting to avoid his questions, she
pushed up to touch his lips with hers.

Her gaze fell to the inside of his lower arm, and
she nodded toward the small tattoo. "What does it
mean?"

Jack groaned, but a tentative smile pulled at the
corner of his mouth. "Ex Nihilo Nihil Fit. 'Work hard,
play harder' in Latin, or, well, a little closer to the mark;
'Out of nothing, comes nothing.'"

At her questioning gaze, his smile bloomed.
"From my Alaska days. A bunch of us flew into
Anchorage for the weekend and I was a little buzzed …

well, we all were. At least my choice was a little more tasteful for lack of a better word. Some of the other guys chose … poorly."

"Oh? Like how poorly?" Curious, but thankful for the subject change, she ran a finger over the delicate script.

He flushed. "Well … that was a long time ago."

"Mmhm." She poked his side and he recoiled. Of course, she did it again, her own smile broadening.

"Fine, okay. Let's see, one guy got a skull with tentacles…"

"All right. A little juvenile, but what else?"

"One got 'Mom' with a heart."

"*Seriously?*"

"Yep. I guess he was a traditionalist."

"And…?" Amused, Sky watched the red creep up his face again.

"Let's just say he had a Double D breast fetish."

She blinked. "How *charming*. Oh, well. I guess he wouldn't be giving someone like me a second glance then."

Jack's face changed again and it was her turn to flush. A playful, but wolfish grin transformed his features, his eyes glittering. "Eh. Sometimes more than a handful can be wasteful."

"Nice to know that not every man on the planet only finds beauty in voluminous cup size.

He shrugged. "I'm equal opportunity."

When Sky laughed again, he leaned in and kissed her, soft and sweet. When he pulled away, regret crunched his face. "I don't want to sound like that *kind* of guy, but I probably should get going. I have an appointment with the silver fox of Meadowbrook Elementary."

She quirked a brow at him and he grinned.

"Actually, it's Avery's teacher. Mrs. Carlisle is sweet, fair, stern when necessary, and about a hundred and five."

"Well then. I can't be responsible for keeping you from such an important meeting." She smiled, but it faded. "Is Avery okay?"

"Yeah, she's fine. She was having some problems earlier and although it seems things have settled down, it's kind of a follow-up. That and grade type stuff." He kissed her again. "Did you want to get together again this weekend? You can come by my place. I know Rosa is dying to cook for you."

"Um ... uh ... how about this? Didn't you promise me a trip to the drive-in? Wouldn't Avery enjoy that?"

"Sure, we can do that. I'll conspire with my offspring. We could swoop by and pick you up. Sound good?"

"Sounds great."

The tiny part of her entangled in superstition shrieked in alarm at her for crossing the line, but she batted it away like a persistent gnat. Sky only hoped it wouldn't come back to bite her.

Chapter Twenty-Three

Stephen let Benny drive. He couldn't trust himself to walk straight, let alone drive his truck. His concentration was shit.

He'd considered calling Sky, but figured it would be better to wait. Other than exchanging some friendly, teasing texts (she kept mentioning Jack, just to get a rise out of him), they hadn't had much contact. Even if he managed to avoid telling her of his discovery, she knew him well enough to suspect something was up. He just couldn't go there. Not yet.

Leaning over, he changed the music for the third time in five minutes. During the last thirty miles, he'd gone from Nirvana to Conway Twitty to Linda Ronstadt to AC/DC to Pink to Def Leppard to The Carpenters to Dueling Cellos.

"Touch that one more time and, dude, I'm going to break your fingers." Benny turned his head with a huge smile beneath his aviators.

"Oh. Sorry." Stephen leaned back, his right knee vibrating. He'd told Chloe he and Benny were going up to Deep Fork to do some fishing, camping out, and then heading home the next day. It was something more to feel guilty about.

It had taken longer than he'd anticipated just to get to this point. He didn't know he had to be on some approved visitor list. This shit was all new to him. But Benny had been right—she'd agreed to see him. Of course, this information came through the official chain only.

He just needed to get through the next couple hours without turning himself inside out.

"So, when you gonna ask Chloe to marry you?"

Stephen turned to squint at his friend. "Seriously, man? You're bringing this up now of all times?"

"Seems like the perfect time to bring it up." Benny grinned again without taking his eyes off the road. "You know she's perfect for you. And she's not gonna wait around forever."

"We like things the way they are."

"Oh, I don't know. I heard she told Daisy Silver, who told Dave Childs, who told Agatha Roundhouse that she wanted some commitment already."

"We *are* committed." Steve grimaced. "Sorta."

"Mmhm. I understand Jordan Cable is back from the air force. Didn't they use to have a *thing* in high school?"

"*What?*"

"Weren't they like high school sweethearts or something?" Benny's tone was matter-of-fact and Stephen felt himself bristle.

"That was forever ago."

Benny lifted and dropped a shoulder. "History repeats. I heard he came into the Kwik Stop and chatted her up."

"*Are you shitting me?*" Something leapt through his insides, something a little too close to jealousy for comfort.

"Yeah, I'm shitting you."

Stephen stared at him, blinked. "You asshole."

"Yep. How 'bout we stop for a burger? We're almost at the halfway point."

****

At the parking lot checkpoint, Stephen and Benny stood solemn as guards searched the truck. They peeked beneath the seat, in the glovebox, and used a mirror to check the undercarriage of the vehicle.

Except for the perimeter, the prison didn't look

like anything from a movie, as far as Stephen was concerned. It looked like a huge, interconnected office building with a red brick façade, surrounded by tall, barbed wire fencing.

With an okay from the guards, Benny drove through the checkpoint, finding parking not far from the visitor's entrance. There were more cars than Stephen would have figured. He berated himself a moment later for the stupid thought. Most incarcerated people had folks on the outside who loved them, despite poor choices.

"Steve?"

Blinking, he turned.

Benny had cut the engine and now stared at him. "You want me to come in or wait out here?"

"Um…" He couldn't think, his knee continuing to jitter. It all seemed so surreal. Colors were too bright, movements seemed stuck in a gliding haze. Looking down, he expecting to see comic book lines emanating from his knee, like he was just a picture on a page. Meanwhile, his stomach pulled itself tight, unyielding. He hoped to hell he didn't puke again.

"How about I come in with you initially? I'm sure you'll have several airlocks to go through, so I'll just hang in one of the outer ones." At Stephen's distracted nod, Benny pulled himself from the cab, pausing before he shut the door. "You ready, man?"

Stephen pulled in a deep breath, the knot in his stomach not easing. He wondered if he should have brought a plastic bag. "Yeah. Let's go."

They pushed in through the front entry. Directly before them stood another checkpoint with a walk-through metal detector. To the right was a small waiting room with a row of plastic chairs attached to the floor. In a wall-mounted rack, magazines protruded from their slots. Stephen caught glimpses of *Field & Stream, Texas Monthly,* and *Better Homes and Gardens.* A soda machine stood perpendicular.

Without saying a word, Benny smacked his bicep and walked over to peruse the reading selection. He found a *National Geographic* tucked behind one of the others and chose a seat.

On autopilot, Stephen followed instructions, showing ID and leaving his phone and keys in a small plastic bin to be picked up on the way out. He walked through the metal detector, allowing a pat down by a male guard.

He was directed to another room, a long one separated into smaller rooms not all that much bigger than phone booths. Each one housed a plastic chair, a metal desk bisected by a clear acrylic wall, and a phone hanging on the right of each partition.

"Here. You'll be in room six. Your family member will be out shortly." The guard opened the door and waved him forward, her voice courteous, even warm.

"Thank you." Stephen slid into his seat, crossing his arms to rest on the cool metal and faced the plastic barrier. He studied the cross-hatching of wires embedded in the acrylic.

This was all wrong. She shouldn't be here.

His eyes burned and he blinked quickly. It was imperative that he keep it together. He'd always been known for his stoicism and now was the time he needed to tap into that aspect of his personality. His knee started jiggling and he stilled it with effort.

On the other side of the partition, he heard a door open and close from the far end.

A moment later, a guard appeared, escorting an inmate dressed in a white jumpsuit.

Stephen stood up to face her, his breath sticking.

The middle-aged woman was tiny and fine-boned, with dark hair running with rivers of gray. It was just long enough to touch her collarbone. Despite her hair, save for a few fine lines, her face looked smooth. Eyes the color of bittersweet chocolate stared into his.

His eyes.

He lowered to his chair, reaching for the phone with a shaking hand, while she did the same.

He heard her rush of breathing first, reminding him to pull in some air himself. With a voice distant from his own, he greeted her. "Hi, Mama."

"Hello, sweetheart."

Chapter Twenty-Four

Stephen watched his mother's eyes overflow and she swiped tears away with the heel of her hand. "You've grown into a very handsome man."

Thick acrylic and almost twenty-five years separated him from this woman, but as he gazed at her, time fell backward. She'd been young and beautiful, the loving mother quick with a kiss, warm hug or a treat. She'd helped with homework, did crafts with them, walked them to the park, patched knee scrapes, patiently listened to their rambling stories, and rocked him when he was small.

When she wasn't cowering.

Stephen stared at the ceiling, blinking to control his emotions. He looked back at her to find her watching him before her eyes flicked beyond him and back.

"Your sister doesn't know." There was no question in her words.

Without hesitation, he shook his head.

"You're still protecting her." She allowed a gentle yet sad smile. "I haven't seen any recent photos of either of you. Your grandmother sent me your school pictures, but she said new ones were almost like trying to catch a photo of Bigfoot."

He laughed, despite circumstances. It sounded like something Mawmaw would say.

"When did you find out about me, Steve?"

The quiet question sobered him and he sighed. "I found your letters. Mawmaw must have kept every single one. She bundled them up and stuck them at the bottom of a keepsake box. She also wrote a letter to Sky and me, telling the full truth. At least, I think it's the full truth. All this time, she knew you were alive but kept it from us."

Sadness pressed into her pretty features and guilt stole through him. The edge to his own voice surprised him, but his emotions were too close to the surface, something he never really allowed.

He hated feeling out of control, but there was little about this situation he could change. Taking a breath, he shut his mouth, fearful what else might come out.

****

Nita watched her son for a long moment, hearing his bitterness, knowing his struggle. "She did exactly as I asked. Honey, even at twelve years old, you wouldn't have let me do what I needed to do. It was better that you both believed I was dead."

"Mama—"

"No, Stephen, you need to listen."

He quieted, his dark eyes locked on hers. Even as a child, he'd been her intense one. Skylar had been stubborn, but she'd also been freer with her laughter, at least in the beginning. Nita felt a pang, longing to see her daughter, unsure if it would even happen. Pushing the fear aside, she concentrated on her firstborn.

"I refused to let you pay for my mistakes. I turned my back on your grandmother and my home. I was young, but I won't consider that an excuse. Your father was handsome and so full of charisma, but my mother warned me. Her instincts were correct, of course, but I wouldn't listen to her, even resented her for trying to ruin my life. I thought I was in love and mature enough to make my own choices. Typical teenage BS. When I left home, I was already pregnant with you. We relocated hundreds of miles away and only then did John Patrick begin to show his cruel side. But I was stuck. I was too ashamed to go home, so I pretended everything was fine. He'd go in waves. After he'd hurt me, he'd cry and beg forgiveness. I forgave him because I didn't know what else to do. Of course, soon he didn't even bother to apologize."

A muscle pulsed in Stephen's jaw. He didn't interrupt though.

"And then I found myself pregnant again. Part of me was so excited, but I was mostly terrified. John Patrick had always been possessive, but he'd become even worse. He'd become interested in certain … dark subjects … some version of witchcraft from what I could figure. I know it's crazy, but he read everything he could on it, even slipping away to meet others with similar *interests*. He was deadly serious about it and I was afraid if I tried to leave, he'd kill me, or worse, kill you. So I continued to pretend. We were a normal family with normal family spats. The fact that I'd had to sometimes use concealer to hide bruises didn't matter. I even had an intuitive neighbor lady try to talk to me about the *accidents* I couldn't erase with makeup, but I denied everything and avoided her."

Nita leaned forward, clenching the phone, trying to relax her grip. "That night, you were forced to do what I couldn't. I should have figured out some way for us all to escape before it got to the point it did, but I didn't. As a result, my child was put in an impossible situation. You did what you did to save your sister. And I'd be damned if I was going to let you pay for it." She pushed the last few words through her teeth, the familiar self-hatred flaring.

Wide-eyed, Stephen stared at her for a full minute, before dropping his gaze and swallowing. "A friend of mine told me that mothers will do anything to protect their children. I do understand, but this is above and beyond. I mean, you've lost years…"

"It doesn't matter. I would still make the same

choice now. The fact that the two of you have grown into fine people is my reward." Nita shook her head, happy he didn't bring up his father's odd interest. He probably didn't even know what to say about that. "You're compassionate, kind, and educated, from everything your grandmother told me."

"Especially Sky."

"My daughter, the almost doctor." She rolled the idea around in her head. Nita pictured a kindergartener giving her a sticky kiss after sampling cotton candy at some street fair off the freeway frontage.

"She graduated in the spring, so she is officially Dr. Donaghue now." He smiled and shook his head, as if in amused denial.

"It's hard for me to fathom. Is she working in the field or teaching?"

A cloud passed through his eyes. "She's done both, but she's teaching right now."

"Is something wrong?" A blast of icy fear brought back another time and she squelched it.

He shook his head, but seemed more reticent now. "I also know about your parole date, Mama."

The guard appeared behind her, the woman's voice barely audible, and Nita nodded. Time was almost up.

"That's not for another few months."

"I'll be here. You need to come home."

Tears burned in her eyes and a sob passed her defenses. "We'll see, Stephen."

He reached out to lay his hand flat against the acrylic barrier.

After a moment, she did the same, startled to see how much bigger his hand was than hers. A grown man. Thirty-six years old, thirty-seven in December. *Her son.* Sky would be thirty, thirty-one next June. *Her baby girl.*

Almost twenty-five lost years.

"Thank you for coming to see me." She started to hang up the phone, but paused. "I'm glad you found those letters. I'm selfish enough to admit that."

She hung up and the guard escorted her away from her son.

Chapter Twenty-Five

They'd finally gone to the drive-in and Jack had watched as Skylar raced to the swings with Avery, both laughing. He wanted to witness moments like that the rest of his life and had taken a mental snapshot of the two of them as the first one to savor.

He just didn't remember her decision to come home with him, but in the murkiness between awareness and slumber, he didn't question. Sky was here now, nestled in his arms.

Soft light from a yellow-orange moon sifted between the blinds to illuminate the pale skin of her shoulder and neck. Jack blinked sleep irritated eyes and curled against her from behind. Silky hair tickled his nose and he breathed in the fragrance of vanilla and peaches.

"Skylar." He mumbled, voice rough long before the dawn. Jack pushed the strap of her nightie down to press his lips to her smooth flesh. A breathy moan escaped her and he moved closer, not wanting any distance between her body and his.

Abruptly, she shifted away from his touch, sitting up to slide her legs over the edge of the bed. The sheet and blanket fell from her form when she rose to her feet and glided across the carpet. Dark waves tumbled down her back and across her shoulders.

Ice formed in Jack's chest and lungs. He couldn't catch a breath around it when he scrambled backward across the mattress, a cry dying inside.

Not Skylar.

Vanilla and peaches.

Nikki.

At the doorway, she turned to face him. She

appeared as she did the day they met, the day they'd huddled together in the bus shelter against the sudden onslaught of Texas rain. So young. So beautiful. "You said we were forever."

Opening his mouth, he tried to find words. Any words. But the constriction inside wouldn't even allow a whisper. All he could do was shake his head in horror. *Please.*

She stared at him, her features soft and sad.

"I loved you," Jack croaked, the words ripping at the inside of his throat.

The corners of her mouth pulled down and her image blurred but didn't dissipate. She turned to leave the room, pausing, as if in indecision, before moving up the hallway.

Jack's paralysis broke into the pins and needles of a dead limb, but he forced himself to leap from the bed, barely conscious of the cooling sweat on his bare chest breaking into gooseflesh. "Nikki!"

He pursued the figure into the living room, to find her gone.

Breathing hard, he glanced around. All he heard was the ticking of the miniature grandfather clock on the mantle and the hum of the refrigerator from the kitchen. The glow of a nightlight shown from the hallway, but shadows remained heavy around him.

Stilling, he waited.

Nothing.

"Christ." Jack ran a hand through his hair. When was the last time he sleep walked? When he was eight or nine? He wasn't even sure.

Sighing, he wandered into the kitchen, turned on the light above the stovetop, and grabbed a glass to fill with fridge water.

Jack gulped down the water to sooth his dry

throat. He turned toward the sink, only to see Nikki's shadow rush him, hands outstretched, claw-like. In the dim light, he saw her face mangled, one side crushed, shards of bones piercing from the flesh. Half her body appeared distorted, as if her skeleton had been twisted around only to be ground to powder, leaving sagging flesh, tearing under the strain. Nikki looked like the car crash victim she'd been. Voice lost, he dropped the glass and fell back against the door of the refrigerator, rocking the big appliance.

The image disappeared as quickly as it had appeared, leaving Jack gasping, eyes wide and searching. A shattered glass in a small pool of water lay at his feet.

"What the fuck?" His recovered speech was hoarse and shaking in his ears. *"What the fuck?"*

****

Jack sat in the center of his couch, his legs stretched across the coffee table, nursing a bottle of ale. It was a little stronger than what he normally drank, especially at three in the morning.

He knew it had just been a nightmare, but damn, it had left him shaking and unnerved. Cognitively, he knew his mind and heart were battling between his past love and his … current one. Lend to that, a vivid imagination that had conceived several horror novels and what could he expect?

Thinking about Skylar again, his heart kicked into overtime and he shook his head.

When had it happened?

Could he pinpoint the exact moment he fell in love? Was it possible he'd started that first day in the park? Or even on the staircase? Maybe. If he believed in that sort of thing. Most likely it was a collection of lovely moments they'd shared over the last couple of months. Either way, the other night at the drive-in had cemented it. They'd finally managed to get there after talking about it for weeks. Avery had dozed off during the second feature, curling into Sky. She'd put her around the little girl, casually stroking her hair. Jack wasn't sure she'd even been aware of the very maternal reaction.

He had no other words for the emotion rising and falling over him. He didn't think he'd been capable of falling a second time.

For once, Jack was happy to be wrong.

"Daddy?"

At Avery's choked sob, he looked up and lurched to his feet immediately. Without any thought, only instinct, he swooped the child into his arms, holding her close as she buried her face against his neck, body trembling. His heart accelerated in empathetic panic. "What's the matter, honey? What happened?"

"He was in my room."

"What?" He gripped her tighter. "Who was in your room?"

"The burnt man." Her voice choked on her words.

Jack relaxed, just a fraction. "A nightmare?"

She shrugged, still clinging to him, grip fierce.

"Shall we go look?"

Avery shook her head, her bed head of waves brushing his jaw. "He smells bad. He says she's supposed to come home. She's meant to come home and bring her brother to him."

"Who's supposed to come home?" Perplexed, Jack tried to look at her, but she held on too tightly, pushing her hot and sweaty face into the side of his neck. "Avery?"

"I dunno," she sobbed. At one time it would have elevated to a wail, but she was slowly adopting an older child's deep, anguished cries that balanced between internal and external. "He's really mad though."

"How about you wait here and I'll go look." Jack walked back to the couch, but when he tried to unwrap her arms from around his neck, she refused to let go. "Okay, then. We'll go together. You just keep your eyes closed."

"'Kay." Another shrug was followed by a violent shudder.

Frowning, Jack stalked up the hallway and flipped on the overhead light in the girl's bedroom. Sebastian, the guinea pig, hid in his hut, not bothering to come out and stare at them, but from what he could tell, nothing appeared amiss. He pulled in a deep breath through his nose, but didn't detect anything other than the subtle scent of cedar, Avery's new watermelon shampoo, and the telltale sign of a rodent cage.

"There's nothing in here, baby."

"He disappeared. He was like smoke."

He rocked her gently, his mind tumbling back to when she was a colicky infant. Many nights he'd paced with her to give Nicole a small break. "I think you just had a nightmare, honey. As scary as it was, it can't hurt you. And you know what?"

"What?" Avery sniffed.

"I had a nightmare too. Maybe it's because Halloween is coming up. What do you think?"

Avery didn't respond for a long moment. When she did, her question was tentative and wavering. "Daddy, can I please sleep in your room tonight?"

Wincing, Jack remembered being kicked hard in the kidney under similar circumstances just before they'd relocated. "Won't Sebastian be lonely?"

"He'll be okay."

Well, hell. "Just tonight, Avery."

Chapter Twenty-Six

Stephen's text was terse, without a hint of sarcasm or normal brotherly teasing.

Skylar, call me when you can.

Sky had frowned at the message, concern heavy and uncomfortable in her stomach. She'd let her last morning class out a little early so she could hurry up to the teacher's retreat. Jack was supposed to meet her up there for an early lunch and she hoped to talk to her brother before he arrived. With any luck, no one else would be up there.

She dashed up the stairs, glancing over her shoulder to make sure no students were paying attention, before pushing through the fire door.

Despite a calendar claiming autumn, the day was already warm. Dark clouds accumulating to the west promised at a possible shower or two later. Sky hoped so.

Someone had recently lugged a patio table and chairs up the stairs and onto the wide balcony. A faded blue and white umbrella jutted from the center, shading a few faculty members who sat around it chatting and smoking.

Disappointed, Sky nodded to them regardless and retreated to a far corner with a view and a little more privacy.

There was no guarantee she'd even get a hold of Stephen. Mondays were always busy at the garage. More than likely, she'd leave a message and they'd proceed to play phone tag for the next several hours.

He startled her when he picked up after the second ring. "*Halito*, Sky."

"Jesus, Steve. What's up with that text? You didn't call me 'dork' or 'geek' once. Should I be concerned?" Even as she said it, she sensed his somber mood. He remained quiet, almost like he was trying to find the right words. It reminded her of the day he'd told her about Mawmaw's stroke. A chill flowed through her, even as sweat dampened her back. "Seriously. Is everything *okay*?"

"Um…"

"Steve…?" She could barely get a whisper out.

"Sorry to spook you. Everyone's fine up here, but we just need to talk."

"I'm listening." Sky found her voice again, but it wavered. "What's going on, Stephen?"

He sighed. "Actually, I wanted to let you know I'll be driving down in a couple of weeks. I wanted to come down sooner, but that would screw over Benny and the guys. It's something we should really discuss in person. I just wanted to give you enough of a heads up in case you have any other plans."

Despite assurances, her mind ran to a familiar dark place: *'The doctor found a spot on my lung'* was always at the top. "Is it regarding your health?"

A dry chuckle reached her. "You would think that, but honestly, I'm okay. My ulcer was bugging me a bit, but it's feeling better now. Stop worrying, Sky. It just involves something … um … I found in those boxes of Mawmaw's."

"It's serious enough to drive over three hundred miles to a town you despise?"

"Yeah, it is, Skylar."

Sky blinked at his bluntness, annoyed that he wouldn't tell her anything more. She pulled in a breath and let it out in a slow current. "Well, you're welcome to my couch."

She turned around, noticing the table people had left, but Jack had arrived. Nodding, she held up her index finger. *Give me a second?*

He tipped his head to the side with a smile and set a bag and two drinks on the table. Amused, she watched as he picked up a chair and propped it under the door. He then eased into one of the others and stretched his long legs out before him.

There was an extended pause of the other end that puzzled her. It wasn't like Steve hadn't crashed on her couch here and there when she was in grad school. "Sure. Thanks."

She glanced over at Jack again. He was messing with his phone, unbothered, unhurried.

"All right then. Is there anything I need to know prior to your visit?"

"Like what?"

"I'm not sure … maybe you've turned vegan or developed some weird allergy to books or only drink decaf now. I just want to be prepared." She smiled and figured he could hear it.

"Nah, I'm still the pissy yet charming big brother you love to loathe."

"Ha ha. Give me a call when you're heading out."

"Will do, kiddo. See you relatively soon."

Sky tucked her phone in her purse and joined Jack at the table. Since no one was around, she leaned down to give him a soft kiss. "Hey, there."

"Hey, gorgeous. Everything okay?"

Her face warmed and she sat next to him. "Sure. That was just my brother giving me a heads up he'll be visiting me."

"The same big brother who scared all your boyfriends?"

"The one and the same."

"Swell." His tone was dry and she laughed.

"That's okay. I'll make sure he behaves." Her

smile slipped a little as she studied him. His eyes seemed a little hollow to her. "Are you okay? You look tired."

Jack shrugged and began pulling sandwiches and chips from the bag. "Yeah, it's fine. Avery's just been having some nightmares. Of course, it results in her hogging my bed and kicking me the rest of the night."

"Ah. Poor kid. Poor *you*."

"I think it's just because Halloween is around the corner ..." He paused and made a point of giving her an obvious side eye.

"Well, *that* wasn't suspicious at all." She unwrapped her lunch and took a test nibble of her chicken salad on a croissant.

"And here I thought I was being subtle."

When Sky raised her brows, Jack sighed. "Okay, I need a favor, but I don't think it's the worst favor I could ask of you."

She sipped her Dr. Pepper. "I'm not sure how to respond to that. I think I'm going to need a little more information."

Nodding his head, Jack chewed on the corner of his lower lip. When he finally spoke, his words were rapid fire. "*Okay, okay. I found-out-this-morning-that- I-chose-the-short-straw-and-I've-been-saddled-with-taking-five-eight-year-olds-trick-or-treating. Please-help-me.*"

Staring at him, she took in the panic and the beseeching look in his eyes and promptly burst out laughing. He watched her with a little smile on his lips, although the look of dismay hadn't eased. Sky reined herself in, feeling a little bad. "You really are serious."

Jack nodded again, solemn now. "I'd never lie about being covered in munchkins."

"You just want me to help you *herd* them?" She wondered how much time she'd have to spend in his house. Up to this point, she'd managed to avoid it. They'd either go to dinner after work or Jack and Avery would swoop by and pick her up to go on a day outing. Occasionally, Jack had invited her over, but she'd always managed to find an excuse that didn't sound too much like an excuse.

"Yeah, pretty much." He leaned closer, his aftershave warm but subtle in her sinuses, gaze on hers. "I'd owe you one."

Sky hesitated, knowing she'd finally run out of excuses. With some effort, she smiled and teased. "One? By my count, that would be five."

"Well, maybe we could work something out." He kissed her softly and she sighed into it, lunch and apprehension forgotten.

Chapter Twenty-Seven

Avery left the clearing where she'd spent the last hour reading and made her way back to the house. A month or so back, she'd dragged out her tent and pitched it between a couple big trees just a few yards from the glen. Now, it was her quiet place. She liked listening to the birds and the trickle of water at the bottom of the hill. Besides, it kept her out of the house. Lately, she could swear her bad dreams were pushing into her waking world here and there. Sometimes, she'd see a figure in the corner of her eye, but it was fast enough to make her doubt herself. Her Dad often told her she was cursed with his imagination, so she hoped that was all it was.

She didn't think so though. The nightmares, although infrequent, hadn't gone away. She just didn't bother her Dad about it now. She'd often choose to curl up with her blanket and pillow next to his bed, scooting back to her own room before he woke up. Her belly stayed tense much of the time and occasionally she'd catch a quick waft of something burning. It disappeared just as fast, but it still disturbed her.

Pausing by the back door, Avery tilted her head, listening for Rosa, hearing the vacuum cleaner, knowing she'd be done any minute. She let herself inside, quickly identified the woman's location as her Dad's room and slipped down the hall and into the bathroom.

Her costume was all ready to go. Not that it was much of one. Avery decided to dirty up some old jeans and a sweatshirt, and her Dad bought her some zombie make-up at the Halloween store. Easy, but effective, as her Dad would say.

Baily would arrive soon to help zombie-fy her and in an hour or so, Tina, Ashleigh, and Makayla should be dropped off by their parents. Avery was always excited by Halloween and tonight shouldn't be any different. She just wished she felt better about things.

Dad said he'd invited Sky along, hoping she didn't mind. And she didn't. Not exactly, at least. She really liked the lady, especially since she seemed to make her Dad happy. He'd been sad for way too long. Avery loved hearing him laugh again.

She couldn't help but worry though. Her belly told her something wasn't quite right. She just didn't know what it was.

The doorbell rang and Avery cut off the direction her thoughts had taken.

Baily was waiting.

****

"Your blonde lady is here, Dr. Jack!" Baily bellowed over her shoulder and Avery shushed her.

All five girls were watching from the front window and Jack cringed. He hadn't *really* needed Sky to help him wrangle children. He'd kind of laid it on thick, looking for an excuse to lure her over to keep him company. He was lucky she hadn't caught on. In general, he liked kids. Except for the kid Avery punched. That one he could do without.

He knew he'd fallen too fast and sensing a certain reticence in Sky, new worry had begun seeping into him. Her wariness wasn't always there though. When he kissed her, she returned it with warmth and passion, but whenever he'd invite her to his home, she'd turn skittish. Frankly, Jack was surprised she'd agreed to come by tonight.

Jack opened the door and stepped out onto the front porch, while the kids oozed from behind and around him. "Hi."

Tucking her hair behind one ear, she stopped at

157

the base of the stairs and smiled up at him. "Hi."

The muscles in his legs weakened a little over that smile, but concern shoved aside the lovesick puppy feeling. In the brightness of the porchlight, she looked a little pale to him.

He hopped down the steps and, conscious of five pairs of eyes watching, kissed Sky on the cheek instead of the lips. "You okay?"

"Sure. Is everyone ready?" She brushed him off and split her attention between the zombie, the fairy, the anime character (Jack didn't have a clue which one), Mr. Mistoffelees from Cats (he guessed), and a Hi-C juice box (creative but uncomfortable as far as Jack could tell). Avery zombie growled at her and Skylar growled right back.

"Okay, everyone, listen up." He made eye contact with each kid to let them know he wasn't messing around. "Remember the rules. Number one: We need to stop at my next-door neighbor's first because if she has hurt feelings she won't make me any more chocolate chip banana bread. Number two: Don't get too far ahead. That's pretty self-explanatory. And number three: Don't snack on too much wrapped candy when Sky and I aren't looking. I can't deliver puking children back to their parents. It makes them upset." Jack waved the giggling girls forward with one hand and slid his other one into Sky's, lacing their fingers. Her skin was cold and he cast her a quick glance, which she didn't seem to notice.

The girls dodged around the RV and ran up to Molly's front door, the juice box sadly lagging behind. Jack felt the glow of pride when Avery returned to walk next to ... Tina? At least he thought that one was Tina.

They regrouped under the porch light, gasping and fawning over Mr. Chuckles who appeared first, looking quite dapper in a tux. Molly stood next to him, wearing a straight, short, sequined dress and a beaded headband.

"She looks good as a flapper." Sky returned the woman's wave.

Jack paused, looking down at her. "I didn't know you knew Molly."

"Oh." She blinked, brow furrowing. "Um ... I guess I must have come by to see you a while back and you weren't home, so Molly and I chatted for a bit."

She seemed flustered and after a long moment, he decided to let her off the hook with a gentle tease. "So, you're stalking me now, huh?"

A sigh slid between her lips, ending on a chuckle. "That must have been it."

Jack's gut told him she wasn't being completely truthful with him, and he couldn't figure why. It seemed a weird thing to be disingenuous about. He decided to let it drop. "Molly's an interesting lady."

"She is."

"She's the perfect patchouli or—is it sandalwood?—scented, beaded hippy lady that would horrify my mom." He paused, contemplating. "Maybe that's why I like her so much."

Sky laughed again, the tense moment behind them. "She seems so familiar to me, somehow."

"You said you lived here as a little kid, right? Maybe your paths crossed way back once upon a time."

"Maybe." She looked troubled again, so he hooked an arm around her waist to bring her close to him, kissing the side of her head as the girls crossed the lawn toward them.

"Did you say thanks to Ms. Achen?"

"Of course we did, Dad. We're not heathens," Avery reprimanded.

"But we *are* heathens!" Baily stormed toward the

next house with some kind of banshee wail that made Jack's teeth vibrate.

"She is *so* embarrassing!" Makayla the anime fan commented, scratching under her shaggy, black wig.

"So immature." Ashleigh the fairy and Tina the juice box agreed with deep, serious nods.

"Aw, she's just in the moment." Avery defended as they hastened to follow Bailey.

Jack shook his head with a sigh. "Guess we'd better catch up with the *Little Women*."

He was pleased to see he'd earned another smile from Skylar.

****

The kids had lost most of their exuberance by the time they arrived back on Jack's street. They'd weeded their way through the entire neighborhood, even overlapping into a couple adjacent ones, but denied being tired. The quiet, with an occasional complaint splitting it, said differently.

Sky walked beside Jack, her hand in his. The kids had formed an uneven clump around them, feet dragging but picking up the pace a little when his house was in sight.

The evening had been fun, watching the kids, listening to their banter, and marveling at some of the Halloween decoration they'd come across, but the question around Molly had caused her several moments of disquiet. What she'd told Jack wasn't quite a lie, but it was close enough to bother her. Her dismay was compounded by his expression. It hinted he didn't believe her but didn't want to push either. It gnawed at her, but she just didn't know what else to tell him.

Makayla's parents were waiting for them and Jack gave a wave as the girl found a spike of energy and scuttled forward. Before climbing into the back seat of the sedan, she called out to the other girls.

"Bye, guys! See you at school!"

Avery and her remaining friends scurried toward the front door, waiting expectantly as Jack slid his hand from Sky's and climbed the porch steps to allow the small herd of children into the house. They stampeded inside and he turned to wait. Gazing at her, a slow frown creased his brow.

She didn't return Jack's questioning gaze. She stared beyond him into the house, even as its warm light spilled out to welcome her, a familiar coldness beyond simple temperature settled around her. It pulled the air from her lungs and a muddled fog settled over her. She took a step back and shook her head before she'd even realized it. "I don't think I can…"

Come on kid … it'll make you feel better…

"Sky?"

Get the fuck away from us! She's fine!

She took another step back and Jack trotted down the front steps to stand beside her. Sky shook her head, her chest heaving, oxygen a slow trickle. She never should have agreed to come here. Everything was beginning to crumble. "I'm sorry. I need to leave."

C'mon, just a little more for Daddy…

She couldn't breathe and her muscles trembled. An intense headache flared behind her eyes, but she couldn't quite tell if it was now or then.

"Leave? I don't understand. It's early." He touched her face and she looked up at him. "You look pale. Are you getting sick again?"

"I don't know." Nauseated and a little dizzy, she turned away. Jack caught her by the wrist, his grasp gentle. Staring at the big hand circling her lower arm, her heart galloped. "Please let me go."

She didn't recognize her voice. It sounded unsure

and childlike.

Back off, you little shit. You don't need to protect her all the time. Daddy's here…

A boy's shouts. A woman's voice pleads.

Soon, you'll feel much, much better, little Sky…

"Let go!" Sky's voice trembled with panic, her chest heaving. She couldn't breathe.

Jack released her as if stung, but she couldn't bear to look at his face. She didn't want to see his hurt, her own pain and confusion echoing his. "I'm … sorry."

He didn't try to stop her when she climbed into her vehicle, but she begged a glance in her rearview mirror as she pulled away. Her eyes blurred with unconscious tears and she blinked several times to solidify his image.

Hands shoved deep into his pockets, Jack watched her leave, his expression a mask of shocked bewilderment.

****

Avery watched from the front window, while her friends poked through their evening spoils. She absorbed the odd exchange between her father and Skylar, nodding when the woman left. In that moment, she knew it was for the best. It was safer for Sky. She shouldn't be anywhere near this house.

She tried hard to ignore the sudden rage boiling within her seconds later. She knew it wasn't hers.

Chapter Twenty-Eight

Sky curled on the couch, wrapped in her comforter, and stared at her phone, indecisive.

The panic attack had eased, but she still trembled here and there. Thankfully, her breathing had steadied and the headache had dissipated. She didn't believe a fever was in her future this time. At least, she hoped not. She wanted to talk to her brother to verify what she already knew, but fear of his reaction kept her waffling back and forth. His answer to the whole situation would be simple. Come home and leave this little town in the past for good this time. No looking backward. He'd probably even offer to help her pack again.

It wasn't simple though. That word was barely in her vocabulary these days.

Career aside, she couldn't get Jack's face out of her mind. Not that she could blame him. She'd freaked out and left without any kind of explanation. All she knew was she needed to get out of there. It'd felt as if some unseen force was squeezing the oxygen from her lungs and she sensed, if given the opportunity, it would kill her. Or at least injure her.

From what she could figure, she had two choice. She could gently break things off with Jack, or tell him the truth and watch as he withdrew because he thought she was nuts. Either way, the relationship, as promising as it was, would be over. She wondered if it would be better to be perceived as a bitch or someone mentally unstable, and opted for the former. What made things worse was she knew how hard it had been for Jack to reach out to her and now she'd just stomped all over him.

The phone blurred in her hand and it took several tries to steady her breathing and stem her tears. Feelings burgeoned inside, blazing as if she'd thrown kerosene on an open flame. She cared more for Jack than she dared to analyze. Avery too. To cut them out of her life had become akin to cutting off her own limb and she didn't understand it.

Acting on the floating impulse, she hit Stephen's direct dial, pulling in several deep breaths and swallowing repeatedly to rein herself in. He'd know she'd been crying, but she needed to hold onto some semblance of control.

"Hey ya, lil sis? How you been? When you goin' out with me?" Benny's big smiling voice filled the miles in between them, and Sky felt a wave of warmth and homesickness.

"One week from never."

The usual response would be a belly laugh, but he quieted. "You don't sound so good. It's poker night, but we're taking a break. Steve should be out of the can in a second."

"That's TMI, Ben."

"Yeah, I know. He's here now. Hold on."

Murmurs of male voices clouded the background for several moments before Steve came on. "Hold up, Sky. I'm heading to the other room."

She nodded out of habit, listening to the snick of his lighter, an inhalation, and the burst of an exhalation. Picturing the smoke rising to the ceiling, she closed her eyes.

"What's happened, Skylar? Do I need to come down sooner?"

"No. No, you don't. I just had a question for you."

"All right."

"The house we lived in down here. Was it on Willow Road? Backing to the green belt?" Her words shook even as she tried to steady her voice.

Stephen was quiet for several long moments. "Dead end. Big Elm in front?"

"Mmhm. The garage is off to the side. The backyard is separated from the woods by a chain link fence."

"Jesus Christ. It's still standing?" Shock in his voice reverberated into her. The panic right behind it frightened her even more. "You need to stay the hell away from there, Sky. I'm serious."

She didn't respond, having expected the response.

"Sky?"

"Jack lives there."

****

Sky's lecture went over schedule by just a few minutes, but students waited regardless to ask questions or make comments, thoughtful or otherwise. She tried to give equal attention, but her mind kept drifting. Pulling it back to task, she managed to disguise any lapses and they finally dispersed and wandered away, satisfied with her explanations.

Alone, she packed up her materials, movements automatic and face stoic. Inside, she felt like screaming but didn't want anyone to take notice.

Stephen hadn't told her to break things off with Jack. He wouldn't do that, knowing she'd just push back. Historically speaking, he wasn't wrong. He'd only stressed the necessity to stay away from that house, not bothering to cover up his anxiety when she'd admitted that it seemed to beckon her. She couldn't even explain that part to herself, let alone him.

She slid her phone into her purse, zipped her laptop case shut, and headed for the exit. She desperately wanted to run but feared she'd enter some kind of fugue state and wind up back at that damned house.

He'd sent her a text to enquire if she was okay. It was short and courteous, but Sky could still picture his expression when she drove away that night. A tear or two slid by her defenses and she wiped them away. She'd responded with a simple *fine, thank you* but felt the chill as soon as she hit send. She expected he would too. The pain inside was too real and she'd channeled her energy into her work. Despite personal turmoil, classes still needed to be taught and papers still needed grading.

Deciding to ease her agitation with a trip to the gym, she walked through the classroom exit, stopping short when someone caught her by the arm.

Heart stuttering, Sky didn't think, only reacted. She grabbed the hand, twisted it, and took the edge of hers to push it backward at the wrist.

The man's other arm foundered for purchase, found none, and he went to his knees, face-reddening, mouth-gaping like a landed trout.

Sky released her hold almost immediately and Emerson landed in a heap by the wall, staring up at her, eyes wide.

"Jesus Christ, doc!"

She knew she should apologize, but couldn't quite bring herself to do it. Her heart still galloped like something wild and she took a step back, dimly aware she'd dropped everything the second he touched her. "You scared the hell out of me, Emerson!"

The man pushed himself up, rubbing his wrist, first looking wounded, then flustered. "Sorry. Geez. I just wanted to talk to you before you disappeared for the night."

She just stared at him as he rose, wary about what he wanted, suspecting she knew.

"Remind me to stay on your good side." He grinned at her, despite shock seeping in around the edges.

Most people underestimated her. It was a lifelong annoyance.

"Probably not a good idea to just reach out and grab someone."

"My mistake. I'm sorry. I didn't think." He cleared his throat. "Anyway, I was wondering if you wanted to go out sometime."

"Um…"

"I thought we could go up to Austin, maybe catch a band." His grin pared down to a smirk. "Just don't beat me up or anything."

Saying 'no thanks' was her first impulse. Emerson bordered on obnoxious, and she'd been on the receiving end of many long stares since supposedly ditching him that night at the tavern. It hadn't been even close to a date, but he'd apparently thought otherwise.

But, if nothing else, he'd proven himself harmless. Maybe she should go out. It had to be better than moping at home. All the feelings she held inside were prepared to crush her. Perhaps dodging them by distraction would help diffuse them just a little. Before she could stop herself, she gave him a little smile, unsure how real it appeared. "Sure."

Chapter Twenty-Nine

Restless, Jack spent too much time in his garage punching and kicking the weight bag, but his brain wouldn't shut off no matter how many reps he did. Breathing hard, he rested his hands on his head and wandered back and forth.

For the life of him, he couldn't understand what happened. Skylar had seemed fine while they'd trailed five overzealous kids. She hadn't pulled a dead fish, her grip on his hand soft but firm as they'd strolled. They'd chatted about all kinds of things, including their own childhood Halloweens. She'd shared how she and her brother had decorated their grandmother's home, smiling as she reminisced. She'd laughed over some of his own stories. At least, it had *sounded* genuine.

It had all changed as soon as they'd arrived back at the house. Sky had paled for the second time that evening, and as far as he could tell, she'd had a full-blown panic attack, rushing out like the devil was right behind her only a few moments later.

And now she wasn't returning his calls, only one text. And that text had been cool to the point of barely civil.

He'd seen her in the university library the previous day. She'd been sitting on her own, working on her laptop. Although she'd been concentrating on her task, he could have sworn her expression held the taint of sadness.

Or maybe that's what he wanted to see.

A moment later, she'd looked up, as if sensing his presence, her blue-violet eyes locking his. Something like regret bled into her face and she broke the contact.

With a growl low in his throat, he left the garage

and entered the house through the side entrance. Stepping into the kitchen, he stood listening to the silence.

Avery was over with Bailey again. She seemed to want to go over to her friend's a lot of late, but then again, little girls were little girls. And it was Saturday after all. He was probably reading more into it than what was there.

Jack pulled open the fridge, wondering if he wanted a beer. Three specialty brews met his gaze. One, he knew for certain, would knock him on his ass. It was tempting, but he shut the door and wandered into the living room.

Several books and magazines sprawled across the coffee table. The corner of one caught his eye and he pulled it from beneath a copy of Harry Potter. Having done research in a variety of questionable realms, he recognized the cover, but didn't understand why it was in his living room. Avery must have gone poking through his office and taken it out of pure curiosity. It certainly wasn't something Rosa would touch.

Irritated, he tucked it under one arm and went to return it to the small bookcase next to his workstation. He'd have to talk with Avery about staying out of his research area. Books on the occult weren't for the squeamish and they especially weren't for children.

He replaced the volume, staring when he noticed some of the other books were out of place. Irritation bloomed into anger and he took several moments to reorder, breathing slowly, carefully. For the first time, Jack was glad Avery was away. When he sat down with her tomorrow, he'd be calm. Just not now.

Pacing, Sky's face entered his mind's eye yet again.

She hadn't just broken his heart, she'd skewered it. He almost laughed at his own stupid sense of hyperbole, but shook it off. Didn't she at least owe him an explanation? Wouldn't that be the right thing to do?

Making his decision, he headed for a shower.

It was still early enough to make a house call.

****

Disaster may have been a kind word to use to describe the previous night's date with Emerson. She should have figured as much when she chose to ignore her instincts.

At least the food was excellent and the band was good. That went without saying. It *was* Austin after all. The company, well, left something to be desired. She determined Emerson certainly liked to talk about himself and all his goals. Quite a lot, in fact. He'd steamrolled her more than once when she'd attempted to respond. He'd laughed a little too loud and drank a little too much. On more than one occasion, he'd tried pushing her to order something with a "higher fun meter."

It had been a long night and one she'd had the pleasure to drive back from. Sky had dropped Emerson off at his apartment, managing to avoid his hands and a goodnight kiss. Then she'd proceeded to drop his car off at the University and retrieve her own. She figured he could grab a Lyft or something in the morning.

The thing was: Emerson wasn't a bad person. He just wasn't what she wanted. In fact, she suspected he wasn't what many women wanted.

And he most definitely wasn't Jack.

Now, Sky curled in the corner of her sofa in pajama bottoms and the "Chahta hapia hoke!" sweatshirt Mawmaw gave her a few years ago, not watching the classic movie on television or reading the book that was splayed in her lap. She'd read the same paragraph three times and when she'd tried to watch the movie, she found herself lost after the first fifteen minutes. She'd never had a problem with being alone before, but tonight the little house echoed with her disjointed thoughts.

Agitated, she stuck the bookmark back in the paperback and tossed it on the coffee table. The movie continued unhindered for movement and noise, while she got up and paced.

Maybe Stephen was right. She shouldn't have come down here. If she hadn't accepted the teaching position, she wouldn't be tearing herself into little pieces. She would have remained ignorant of that damned house and its implications.

And she would have never met Jack.

Pressing her lips together, she felt the bite of tears. Life has never and would never agree to fairness, so what right did she have to expect it? Why should she be special enough to go beyond her own accomplishments and obtain personal happiness too? It was way too much to ask of the universe.

Sky opened the fridge, gazing at a slim selection of orange juice, skim milk, condiments, and two sad avocadoes. Her emergency chocolate supply had been extinguished after last night's "date." She pushed the door shut, harder than she'd intended, rocking the ceramic cookie jar on top. The bear tipped over before she could catch it, shattering against the tile floor.

Numb, she stared at the destruction at her feet, before crouching down within it. Tears she'd been pressing back erupted, running in rivulets and dropping onto the broken shards. Her hands blurred as she gathered large pieces and nested them together.

When did everything turn to shit for her? She'd come down here full of excitement and hope, and now she felt so damned lost. Even worse, she felt helpless, and that was something she hadn't felt since childhood. Figuring she'd had more than her allotment, she hadn't expected to ever feel that way again.

Continuing to cry, she rose, stepping carefully, returning a second later with a dustpan, brush, and paper bag. Gathering the pieces, she disposed of them one by one, sucking in a quivering breath and swearing when a sharp edge nicked the pad of her index finger.

The doorbell rang and she swore again.

She quickly dispensed of the mess and ran her finger under the kitchen tap, drying it with a paper towel and crossed to the front entry. Her mind and eyes fuzzy from crying, she opened the door without thinking.

Jack stood on the other side of the door and she blinked several times, trying to clear her vision. His brows were drawn together in a scowl. His face was angles, shadows, and full of anger, but as they stared at one another, his fury eased. A more natural expression of concern peered out from the anger, extinguishing it completely. "Are you okay?"

She hugged the side of the door, wanting to step into his embrace but refraining. "If you must know, I just broke my Mawmaw's bear. What are you doing here, Jack?"

The ridiculousness of her comment made her want to smile through her tears, but she didn't dare.

He just looked puzzled. "May I come in?"

Sky knew she needed to tell him no. She'd expected they'd eventually come face to face—it *was* a small town after all—and she'd prepared to tell him it just wasn't working for her. It was an egregious lie because she wanted him more than ever, but it needed to be done. She had no choice. Instead, as if on autopilot, she nodded.

Jack stepped past her and she caught the whiff of soap and deodorant. He sported a couple day's stubble and his hair was damp from a recent shower.

"Is Avery okay?" She shut the door behind him.

"She's fine. She's staying over with Bailey tonight. She seems to do that a lot lately."

"Bailey. Mr. Mistoffelees, I believe."

"Yeah, Mr. Mistoffelees." Jack repeated in a murmur.

They were falling into a familiar, comfortable exchange, but she couldn't allow it. "I'm sorry I wasn't clear with you. Things have been a little hectic."

"You didn't even try to be clear." He gazed into her eyes, a spark of his initial anger returning. "Everything *seemed* to be fine. You and I *seemed* to be fine. And then you practically lay rubber outside my house Halloween night and that's that. Do you think you can help me understand? I think I deserve it, don't you?"

"Of course you do." Tears tried to return and she gritted her teeth against them.

"Are you married?"

"Of course not." She stammered, shocked.

"Are you going to say 'It's not you, it's me.'?" Because if you are, I'm going to blow a blood vessel right here in the middle of your living room." His words bit out at her, demanding truth when she couldn't give it to him.

Sky opened her mouth and closed it again. That had been exactly what she'd been about to say, as clichéd as it was. It wasn't a lie though. "I ... I don't think I can explain."

He smiled, but it wasn't a pleasant one. "You can't explain. Now, that's just awesome."

Saying nothing, her heart stuttered in her chest. *So damned unfair.* She didn't want him to hurt. She wanted to put her arms around him and pull him close. An alien, yet deep-reaching emotion had taken hold, but she didn't dare look too close. Not now. Instead, Sky just stood rooted to her living room floor.

Jack shook his head and turned from her to step toward the door. He stopped and she watched his shoulders heave as he pulled in one full, slow breath after the other. Frustration, and confusion radiated off him in furious waves and if he were anyone else, alarm would have already risen inside her.

She gasped when he spun toward her and closed the distance in two long strides. Before she could react, he'd cradled her face in his elegant hands and pressed his lips to hers.

Chapter Thirty

It wasn't a gentle kiss. It was hard and full of frustration, but it didn't matter. Maybe it was instinctive or maybe, despite the supernatural chasm, it was fated, but she returned his kiss without pause, parting her lips, allowing him a more passionate access. A small but fading voice inside whispered she could still stop. It wasn't too late. Ignoring it, she curled her hands in the front of his shirt, holding tight.

His fingers slid down and away from her face, and his arms slid around her waist to lock her close. He nipped and then he soothed. After a few seconds, he grazed his teeth down the side of her neck, shifting to suck and nuzzle her throat, bringing butterflies of sensations throughout her body.

A moment later, he pulled away, wide-eyed, and a chill moved in to replace his warmth. "Oh my God, I'm so sorry. I would never ... I didn't want to make you cry."

She blinked at him and reached up to touch her cheeks, not realizing she'd been crying yet again. That's all she seemed to do these days. She didn't used to be such a ninny. Of course, she'd never been in love before either. Sky quickly buried the thought.

His body shaking, Jack backed toward the door, horror still embossed on his face. He shook his head. "I'm going to go. I'm sorry. I won't bother you again."

****

Jack turned from her, muscles quaking and heart bursting. He wasn't sure when she'd become an addiction. Was it the very first time he'd laid eyes on her on the staircase in the main hall? That day at the park? Something as silly as simply having lunch with her? Or was it the first time they'd made love?

It didn't matter. An addiction could be curbed. The intense love he felt would eventually fade to a tender bruise from the open wound. He had no right to invade her home and demand what she couldn't or wasn't willing to give.

He'd been so agitated since Halloween night, continually weighing whether or not to confront her. His trip here tonight had been impulsive, cresting on the last several days of raw, painful emotion. He'd expected to have his say and give her a chance to explain or at least reiterate her choice. Now he just felt lost.

He reached for the doorknob, hesitating when her low voice reached him.

"Don't go, Jack."

Confused, he shifted to face her. When she taught, she always dressed in skirts and heels, her hair pinned up. She was impeccably elegant—beautiful and just a tad aloof. He figured she was the subject of many a young man's wet dreams, but he doubted that would have ever entered her mind. Today, she wore her hair straight instead of wavy. It hung like silk over her shoulders and without makeup, she looked younger, somehow smaller. Vulnerable.

Shame burned through again, but her eyes kept him locked in place. Those brilliant, haunted eyes shining with tears, but as he gazed at her, a new light entered them, somehow determined, then angry.

"I don't understand, Sky. I've been trying think of anything I could have possibly done, but it's useless. Maybe I'm just pathetic, but I still don't understand anything."

"It's okay." She walked toward him. For a long moment, she studied him, tiny expressions passing through her eyes and over her face.

At one time, he thought he could read her, at least a little. Now he had no clue.

"Trust me. You're not alone." Her whisper carried an unfamiliar rawness, as she pushed up on her toes to kiss him, nibbling the corner of his lower lip in the process. She then took a half-step back, watching him. "Stay with me tonight."

They stared at one another, gazes locked.

Maybe he just wasn't strong enough, but something inside snapped like a rubber band stretched beyond its limit. Primal need, want, and, beyond that, intense love, coursed through him. He caught her around the waist, slamming her body against his, mouth suddenly ravenous as it met hers in possession. Every extraneous thought funneled from his mind and disappeared into smoke, leaving only Sky. Her perfume, the way her fingernails now scraped his shoulders, and the tickling of her hair as it brushed his face whirled around him, securing her in this tiny speck of the world with him.

Sky's fervor matched his own, her fingers seeking access under his t-shirt. She broke the kiss only to pull the garment over his head to discard it. Her lips reconnected with his, mouth hot, tongue aggressive.

Flipping her against the wall, he caught her hands, raising them above her head and held her delicate wrists in one fist, while the other sought the softness hidden beneath her top.

****

Sky couldn't seem to catch her breath, between the passion of his kisses, the touch of his hand against the bare skin of her midriff, and the magnetic heat pulsing from him, she burned with excitement. His arousal pressed against her and she closed her eyes to concentrate on the sensations he summoned in her body, not what the act might mean.

Sneaking his hand under her top, he palmed her breast, his thumb pressing against the nub. A growl of frustration vibrated through him and in one fluid movement, he'd pulled her sweatshirt and sports bra over her head, flipping them aside.

He followed her as she slid down the wall, mouth dropping open, a cry somewhere between a gasp and a scream caught deep in her throat. A thousand fires ignited under her skin when Jack pressed his mouth to her breast, grazing with his teeth, sucking, lapping and returning to her lips with tumultuous passion just shy of brutal.

She was so very tired of the past holding her captive. At least, for now, she allowed all her fear and worries to disappear. Wise or not, it felt *right*.

Continuing to assault her mouth, his hand pressed against her lower belly, fingers poking under the waistband of her pajamas. She arched upward when he stroked and delved, the glide of his fingers finding the perfect pressure. The lingering mint of his exhalations, the taste of his mouth and the firm softness of his skin overwhelmed her senses.

Her bottoms disappeared, her sudden nakedness sandwiched between an area rug and Jack's warm and solid body. His mouth ravaged, sucked, brought her up to that sharp coveted slice of sensation.

When he pushed inside, she met his impact, matching his motions in a graceful dance where each partner knew and anticipated every step. His thrusts powerful, he angled for her pleasure, pounding deep until blackness crept behind her eyes and exploded in a dazzle of lights, her body unfurling with a snap of pleasure. Weakness sunk into her bones as she rode the aftershocks of her climax, her muscles heavy and unable to move.

Sky hardly noticed when his strong arms cradled her, hitching her lank body to his chest as if she weighed nothing. She was floating. That's what it felt like. Blissfully thought and worry free, she floated, before cool sheets hit her fiery skin and Jack held her against him. He smoothed her hair, kissing her with such tenderness tears stung her eyes.

****

She nestled against him, staring at the slices of darkness splitting through the blinds across from her bed. Comfortable and entwined, Sky felt she could stay in his arms forever, but knew she didn't have the right. Her problem hadn't magically evaporated. She'd just pretended it didn't matter and wondered how long she could get away with the pretense. She pressed her lips inward, not willing to allow her emotions to break free again. It didn't help anything.

"What are you thinking?" Jack's low voice made her jump.

"I'm wondering if that was makeup sex for the argument we didn't actually have." She cut her eyes up to him, a smile playing around her lips.

"I did have one hell of an internal argument with you. Does that count?"

"I suppose." She'd hesitated, choosing to smile through her half-truth. "I'm glad you came by.

Serious, Jack studied her and she fought the urge to squirm under his assessment.

"Are you?" He ran his hand over her hair, twisting a strand around his finger. "I feel like you're going to run for it. Is that it? Are you planning on leaving and just don't want to get tied down?"

Bitterness seemed to creep into his voice and Sky felt the now too familiar burn behind her eyes. This would make it easy. She could just acknowledge Stephen was right from the beginning and go home. But…

Jack tipped her chin toward him with his finger and thumb, raising his brows.

Why did the idea of leaving rip a ragged hole through her insides? Had she really been here long enough to make the prospect irreversible?

His blue-grey gaze rested on hers, calm and waiting for a response.

"I … I was never certain this would be permanent." She spoke softly, thankful not to be forced into an actual lie. She'd never been good at it and it wasn't something she cared to hone.

"I know you must miss your family and friends. Moving down here *was* a pretty big change, even if you did live here before."

Oh, God, he was giving her an out. She just couldn't tell if it was inadvertent or not. "I do miss them."

He nodded, still rubbing her hair lightly between his fingers. "I apologize if I came on too strong. It wasn't my intention to scare you off. Maybe, we can just take things little by little. If you decide to go home, well, I won't lie—I'll miss you, but you need to do what you feel is best for you and your family. Now, if you decide to stay—well, we can just play that by ear too, as long as you're all right with that."

"*This* is taking things little by little?"

He shrugged, kissed the corner of her mouth, and lightly nipped her earlobe, chuckling over her unconscious shudder.

Unless Jack decided to move or the vengeful restlessness in the house disappeared, the only thing this did was delay the inevitable. She couldn't be sure if her presence there put her in psychological jeopardy, physical, or both. The only thing she knew, without question, was whatever resided there meant her harm. Jack hadn't mentioned anything about himself or his daughter feeling anything but safe, so it had to be directed only at her. If her father was indeed the entity residing there, he had an agenda, and it didn't involve a happily-ever-after ending for Skylar.

Another shudder reverberated through her body and seemingly knowing he hadn't been the catalyst this time, Jack tightened his embrace. "Cold?"

She shook her head, her gaze flickering across his face, absorbing the details of his handsome visage and the warm intensity of his eyes, as she tried to ignore the agonizing emotion in her chest.

Nestled against him, she wondered what it would be like to stay with him, to just *be*. She let the fantasy play, unwilling to let the real world intrude, at least for the rest of the night. If nothing else, she needed to give herself that gift.

Chapter Thirty-One

When Sky awoke the next morning, the right side of her bed was empty, the sheets cold as if Jack had been gone for a while. Blinking heavily, she gazed over at the bedside clock, 9:02 AM glowing back at her. Not too late for a Sunday. Her hazy, exhausted brain took several moments to note the wonderful aromas reaching her and enticing her stomach to complain at the long stretch without proper food. She couldn't quite remember when she'd eaten last.

With a sudden burst of wakefulness, she threw back the sheets and comforter, wincing at the pain in her body. Three bouts of love-making had left their marks, but the warm contentment inside made it all worthwhile. She refused to think beyond it.

Pulling on her robe, she wandered from her bedroom, finding Jack taking up a lot of space in her small kitchen. He flashed her a grin, teeth white against the darkness of his stubble.

Her belly see-sawed, voice trembling. "Good morning."

If he heard the tremble, he didn't react. "Morning. Um, I hope you don't mind, but I noticed you didn't have any actual food in here. I ran out to the store an hour ago."

"You didn't have to do that." She slipped into the kitchen and he leaned down to kiss her before handing her a mug.

"Sure I did. I needed to show off my culinary skills. It's part of the whole courting thing that birds do, except with omelets, instead of feather displays. Have a seat, breakfast is almost ready."

She laughed, taking her coffee to the little dinette

and slipping onto a cushioned seat. From her location, she watched him plate omelets, hash browns, and bacon, before pouring them juice in tiny Charlie Brown glasses. "Does Rosa know you can cook?"

"I can make breakfast and that's about it. I don't think her title is threatened." He placed a plate in front of her, sliding across from her a couple moments later. Smiling, he locked gazes with her and every memory from the night before warmed her cheeks. She didn't break contact.

A gentle, loving light in his eyes kept her attention and the truth sank in. She didn't know how she knew or maybe it was just a strong intuition, but Jack *loved* her.

Blinking, she looked down at her plate, unsure how to feel. She took a quick breath when unexpected pleasure warmed her, annoyed when her reality threatened push back.

"You okay?"

"Mmhm." She picked up her fork. "Just starving. Thank you for this."

"Anytime."

****

Jack ate quickly, keeping his eyes on Skylar but trying not to be too obvious. He'd been terrified she'd revert back to ambivalence or worse, give a repeat of Halloween. Although quiet, she didn't appear to be heading into either territory, although he couldn't be positive. Sky wasn't exactly predictable. He cleared his throat. "Hey, I'd kind of promised to take Avery on an outing this afternoon. Want to join us for lunch and then skating? Can you think of anything better than continuously skating in circles to loud music and screaming children?"

She hesitated and Jack's heart snuck in a few

extra beats. Maybe she really had made her decision to go home and was just figuring out how to tell him.

Nibbling on a forkful of hash browns, she gazed beyond him, maybe looking at the lush backyard, the frolicking birds or the river gleaming in the early sun. He suspected she didn't see any of those things. She was looking at something he couldn't see. Tension and sadness seemed to press into her lovely features for several long moments before easing. When she shifted her gaze to him, he thought she still looked wary, but her smile wiped the thought away. "That would be fun. As long as Avery doesn't mind."

"Not likely. She loves hanging out with you."

There is was again. A flash of wariness and sadness before the smile. Or maybe he just imagined it because of his own fears.

"Good to know. The feeling is reciprocal." Her smile broadened, easing into every portion of her face and he relaxed a little.

Jack shoveled the last of his omelet in and washed it down with juice. "While I'm thinking about it, I wanted to let you know I have to go to Houston for a couple days next week for a conference. Maybe we could do something that weekend. Or am I overstepping? If you want to take a break, we could do that too."

She shook her head. "It's fine. Maybe I could be the one to plan this time."

"Then I shall leave myself to your more than capable hands." Embarrassment heated his face for a moment, but he grinned at the double-entre.

"*Really?*" Sky rose and stretched, and Jack couldn't keep his eyes from the small, perky breasts pushing against the thin material of her robe. When he managed to look at her face, her brow had raised, amusement dancing in her eyes. Gliding toward him, she straddled his lap to face him. She looped her arms around his neck, pushing down on him to make him groan, an impish smile touching her face when she succeeded. "So, when do we need to leave?"

"Eleven-thirty-ish," he whispered, millimeters from her lips.

"Plenty of time." Skylar caressed his mouth, slow and teasing.

"Mmhm." Jack pressed back, his addictive hunger for her needing no encouragement.

Chapter Thirty-Two

Avery Langham watched her father pack with somber eyes. She knew he'd only be gone one night and be back when she got home from school the next day, but she didn't want him to go. She wouldn't tell him though. His job was important. Plus, she'd acted the baby too much lately. Coming up on nine years old meant she soon would be bumping up against double digits and that was getting close to being a teenager. She needed to act her age.

So now when the burnt man appeared in the shadows, she would shut her eyes and try to shut out his rasping words, telling herself it was only a dream. He'd begun to mention Skylar by name, cementing the worries and suspicions she'd been accumulating. Sometimes when he spoke to her, her brain would feel a little fuzzy. She'd think mean thoughts, but only for a second before they'd go away. Avery knew he wasn't real, but he scared her anyway.

She thought about asking her dad if they could get a dog, figuring a big dog would scare the man away, but remembered the one time when Ms. Achen from next door came by with Mr. Chuckles. As big as he was, he didn't want to come inside.

Not that Avery could blame him now.

"Which do you think?" Her dad held up a deep red tie alongside a midnight blue one.

"The red one."

"Thanks." He put it in his overnight bag.

Rosa would be staying over since Bailey and her family had to travel to New Mexico or someplace for a wedding. It wouldn't be as much fun, but Rosa was nice, even if she could sometimes be bossy.

Maybe Avery would go out to that place in the woods again. As usual, she just had to be careful to time it when Rosa was involved in a long chore, like vacuuming, mopping, or cleaning the bathrooms.

"Are you ready for school?" Dad zipped the little case up and gazed at her. She felt that familiar pull. She didn't remember her mother very well, so her dad was her everything. She always worried he wouldn't come home and almost asked him not to go again, but didn't.

"Mmhm. My backpack's ready. I just need to go get my lunch."

"Well, scoot. I can drop you at school on my way, if you'd like."

"Okay." She wandered into the kitchen to get her lunch.

Rosa was busy cleaning up their breakfast dishes, and Avery tapped her on the arm.

"Yes, *mi sol?*"

"Daddy's taking me to school today."

"All right. You have a good day. I'll see you at the pickup point."

She met her dad at the front door, hesitating when he opened it for her. On impulse, she wrapped her arms around his waist, hugging tight. "I'll miss you, Daddy."

His eyebrows crinkling a little, he pulled her arms from around him and crouched down in front of her. "I'll miss you too, baby, but I'll be back before you know it. You know my number, so ask Rosa if you can use her phone to send me texts. I'll talk to you after school, before you go to bed, and again first thing in the morning, okay?"

"Okay."

He enveloped her in a firm hug and she rested her head on his shoulder. Her dad gave the best hugs. Once, Bailey told her she wished he'd hug *her*, but it was only because she thought he was cute. Although proud of her dad, Avery found her friend's crush a little disturbing.

"Do you think it'd be okay if I called Sky too?" Avery decided it might be time to talk to her about the burnt man. She worried about her coming to the house, but maybe, between the two of them, they could find a way to make him disappear. Maybe they could go to her house and make some plans. After all, it was kind of her fault he was there.

"Um, well, I'm sure she'd love to talk to you." He pulled away and rose to his feet, taking a moment to jot down Sky's number on the notepad he kept on the console table by the entry. He then reached out to tweak her nose. "Just don't make a nuisance of yourself."

"What's that?"

"Basically, don't be a bug. Now, let's go. We don't want you to be late."

****

Sky hadn't been able to do it.

After their night together, Jack remained behind her eyes and in her heart. She couldn't seem to shake her need. Or maybe she'd just given up. As far as he was concerned, she was still on the fence about staying. He wasn't happy, but he'd accepted it grudgingly, willing to wait and see how it all played out.

Which was exactly what she was doing, for better or worse.

Now, as she read and groaned through a paper titled "Indian or Native American? It's all a Point of View," Skylar put it aside when she received a text notification. Jack had left that morning for Houston and would be up to his ears in meetings and presentations, but had promised he'd let her know when he arrived.

Jack: **Well, I'm here. I forgot toothpicks to keep my eyes open though.**

Sky: **I'm sure the hotel can supply some.**

Jack: **Or I can just wear sunglasses and tell them they're prescription. As long as I don't snore, it should be good.**

Sky: **Don't you have a presentation too?**

Jack: **Well, gosh, thanks for the harsh reality.**

Skylar laughed, wishing they were together, once more blocking certain upsetting circumstances. A moment later, he texted again.

Jack: **I hope I didn't overstep ... which I probably did, but it was done in a guilt infused daze...**

Sky: **What did you do?**

Jack: **I gave Avery your phone number. She adores you and I think she was feeling extra lonely with not only me out of town, but her best friend away as well. Sorry.**

A theatrical frown emoji followed his words.

Finding herself strangely flattered, Skylar shook her head with a small smile.

Sky: **It's fine. You know I enjoy talking with her.**

Jack: **Phew, that's a relief. I thought for sure you'd want to punch me in the eye or something.**

Sky: **Don't worry, your eye, along with the rest of you, is safe.**

Jack: **Hmmm ... very good to know. Better get going. Talk to you later.**

Skylar tucked her phone away, turning her attention back to the mess of a paper in front of her. She had seven more after this and had chosen her usual corner of the university library to at least get a few graded. It would be nice to have an on-campus office, but it wasn't in the cards for a new professor, especially an adjunct. She had a ninety-minute two o'clock class to teach shortly, after which, she'd be able to leave, stop at

HEB for a couple of groceries, and then tuck in for the rest of the day and night. With any luck, she could finish grading this batch of papers and actually be able to relax for a bit.

Chapter Thirty-Three

Stephen didn't tell Chloe much of anything. At least, not yet.

She'd come by after work to see him. It had been a study night yesterday, so it was a play night today, but instead of relaxing or doing something much more physical and fun, he watched her pack for him. He wasn't even leaving until the morning, but Chloe did what she did.

It was actually kind of sweet. She was much more efficient, rolling his clothes and keeping like with like. When he packed, he just shoved it wherever. It wasn't like he would be bringing anything dressy to get wrinkled, t-shirts and jeans being his primary wardrobe. Still, he said nothing, not even when she packed more than what he likely needed. Hell, for all he knew, he wouldn't need any of it. Sky may just kick his ass out and he'd be heading home the same day.

"There." She zipped the bag shut and pushed it aside. "Just remember to throw your toiletries in tomorrow morning."

"I think I can handle that—" He almost added a sarcastic "mom" and stopped himself.

She shrugged. "I'm sure you can, but I kind of like doing this stuff for you. Is that weird?"

Stephen gazed at her big brown eyes, pretty features, pouty lips, and shiny hair and felt a pang. *What if she didn't want to have anything to do with him after learning the truth of what he'd done?* "No. It's nice to feel like I'm being taken care of."

A smile pulled at her lips, but it seemed a little strained. She sat on the edge of his bed and studied him. "Are you okay, Steve? You've been a little off for a bit.

Distant. Well, more distant than usual. Is something going on?"

Concern tucked into all corners of her face and that warmth he always felt in her presence burned a little brighter. Yeah, he loved her. There were no doubts and that knowledge scared him more than he could fathom. If he were being honest with himself, he'd always known he'd walked on the edge of a precipice. One false step and he'd lose everything.

God, it hurt so much, but thinking back to that night, what else could he have done? Bringing in the authorities would likely have been a temporary solution. He'd been twelve. The world had been a lot more black and white then. He'd done what he'd felt needed to be done.

And so had his mother.

"Steve?" She got up and stepped close, reaching to cradle his face in her soft hands. "Please, what can I do for you?"

It occurred to him she knew him as well as he knew her. He'd thought he'd always kept his emotions close to his chest and the truth of the realization was startling. "I don't know what to say, Chloe. I did something horrible when I was a kid and the shit is hitting the fan. I mean, the ramifications … well, they were bad before, but, I don't know, they seem even worse now. What's weird, is it shouldn't be worse. Benny pointed out that I have a second chance now."

She took his hand and they both sat on the edge of his bed. "How can a second chance be a bad thing?"

"No, it usually isn't, but when this truth comes out, and it *will* come out now, it's very possible I'll lose my sister." He looked at her, miserable. "Up until now, I just figured the past was the past and there was no reason for her to know everything. It's different now."

He paused, watching her face, seeing curiosity but no expectation. It saddened him a little. She didn't think he'd be forthcoming with her. He decided to be. "My mother is alive."

Chloe gaped at him. "How? I thought…"

"Yeah, so did I. My grandmother left behind a bombshell, and I didn't even know it until recently. I found bundles of letters. Turns out … well … it turns out, she's been in prison all this time." He stopped, eyes burning. His voice strangled in his throat. "She took the blame for what *I* did."

Her mouth trembled, tears forming behind her lashes. "Oh my God, Steve."

She *had* to be reading between the lines, which he was thankful for. He couldn't bring himself to say the words otherwise. He was also thankful she didn't get up and leave.

Sniffling, she wiped her eyes. "Your mother being alive is a gift, Steve."

"It is." He looked down, his shame heavy, malignant. "That's why I'm driving down to Texas. I need to tell Sky everything. I also want to make sure she's okay with my own two eyes. You remember me telling you about those books I found and what I suspected about my father?"

"How could I forget? It made me sick to my stomach."

"Yeah, I know the feeling. What's even more disturbing is my mother basically confirmed John Patrick had grown interested in some kind of dark arts. She said he'd go out somewhere with certain people. People that seemed to really freak her out. Some kind of cult maybe."

Chloe's brow furrowed. "That's beyond terrifying. I'm not sure if I believe in witchcraft or whatever, but, at the same time, I wouldn't want to mess with it. And I certainly wouldn't want to mess with someone who believes in it."

"I hear that." He shook his head. "I'd like to think I'm making more of it than there is. I mean, that was a long time ago and my mother was … well …pretty cowed. The man is dead, after all. But get this— apparently, Sky's boyfriend lives in our old house."

Chloe blanched. "Are you serious?"

"I think so. At least from the description she gave me. What are the fucking odds of that?"

She stared at the wall beyond him. There was a reproduction print from "The Good, the Bad, and the Ugly" hanging there, but he doubted she was looking at that. Pulling her gaze and mind away from her far away thoughts, she focused on him. She kept her words soft. "Do you feel like something is coming full circle? Like something needs to be finished?"

He pushed his hand through his hair, the idea terrifying him, especially knowing Sky felt drawn to their childhood home. Then again, maybe it was simple curiosity, honed by years of listening to other people and their suppositions. "I've thought about it. *A lot,* in fact. But then again, maybe I'm building something from nothing. My worries about some supernatural boogeyman could be just a way to distract me from the fact that my sister may kick me out of her life tomorrow."

Chloe grasped his hand with both of hers, running one gentle thumb across his knuckles. She didn't let go. Her voice shook, but her tone was firm. "That's not going to happen, Steve. Despite what you may have done, you are a good man. There's no doubt about that. Whatever happened all those years ago shaped you to some degree. It's inevitable. But whatever it was, I firmly believe you felt you had no choice. I think maybe you just need to have more faith in Skylar."

"You sound like Benny."

"Do you think we can both be wrong?"

Stephen stared at her for a long minute before smirking. Maybe it was a little half-hearted, but he did it anyway. He needed to lighten the moment or he might implode. "*Of course*, I think you both could be wrong."

She narrowed her eyes and he laughed. Leaning forward, he kissed her. After a playful slap to his bicep, she returned his kiss and they tumbled backward.

In that moment, he made his choice. He'd ask her to marry him as soon as he returned from Texas.

Chapter Thirty-Four

Rosa Cruz peered out the front window, her phone clutched in her hand, her mind whirling. Rain had begun falling, but it remained a drizzle for the moment. Darkness would soon arrive and that combination always scared her. Especially if the skies decided to rip open and deliver a torrent.

It didn't matter though. There was no choice. She'd have to risk it.

She just wasn't sure what to do about the little one. Dr. Jack trusted her with his daughter and she adored the little girl. Most of the time she was a pleasure. She chalked the moodiness of late to just being female. Rosa had raised three daughters, so she knew the drill.

And one of those daughters was currently lying in a hospital room up in Waco. Her son-in-law had called a few minutes ago, crying. There'd been a car accident. The other driver had been going the wrong way.

Trembling, she glanced over her shoulder. Avery was curled in the corner of the couch with her blanket, reading a book. Rose suspected the child was more aware of what went on around her than she pretended. The girl was a smart cookie.

Maybe she should just bring her with her. Her little friend's family was gone for the week and, as far as Rosa knew, the other children were just classmates.

"Rosa? Are you okay?" She'd put the book down and looked up at her, frowning. "You look upset."

She pulled in a shaking breath. "Actually, I am. That was my son-in-law, Michael. My youngest daughter had been hurt in a car accident."

The little girl's eyes widened. "Is she … okay?"

She could have kicked herself, remembering too

late that the girl's mother had perished the same way. Nausea grabbed her as she thought of her own child. "I'm not sure, but I need to go to her. Would you be okay coming with me? I'll call your father before we leave."

Something flashed in the girl's eyes, something silver and somehow menacing. It was gone when Rosa blinked. It was probably just the light.

"We could call Daddy's girlfriend. Maybe she could stay with me."

"Oh. I'm not sure if that's a good idea …"

The girl pouted. "He left her number by the door. Could we at least try? I wanna stay home."

Rosa looked at the time, pressing her lips together, indecisive. She'd heard a lot about Dr. Jack's lady friend but hadn't had the opportunity to meet her yet. Or cook for her.

"Maybe you could call my dad to make sure it's okay."

Nodding, she scrolled her contacts and hit the correlating number for Dr. Jack. She listened to it ring, biting her lip. When he didn't answer, she left a message, rushing in her panic. "I'm sorry to bother you, Dr. Jack, but this is Rosa. I have an emergency. My daughter has been injured in a car accident and I need to go to her. Avery doesn't want to come with me to Waco, but she says your friend, Skylar, might be okay watching her for me. I'm going to call her now. I hope that's okay. Please call me when you can."

She hung up, trying to control her breathing. Rosa looked at the notepad by the door. Skylar Donaghue's number was scrawled in her employer's rushed hand. She punched it in, relieved when the woman answered on the second ring.

"Hello?"

"Hello. Is this Ms. Donaghue?"

There was a pause at the other end. "It is."

"I'm sorry for bothering you, but my name is Rosa Cruz. I work for Dr. Jack Langham. As you probably know, he's out of town right now. I wouldn't have called you, but I didn't know what else to do. It's an emergency—"

"*Is Avery all right?*" The woman cut in, a waver apparent in her voice.

"Yes, she is. She's fine. I'm sorry, I didn't mean to scare you. But my daughter had been in an accident..." Rosa started crying, but choked it back. "She's in a hospital in Waco and I need to go to her. Avery wants to stay home, but … well, I wondered if you'd be willing to watch her tonight. I'm so sorry. I wouldn't normally ask, but there's no one else to call. I left a message with Dr. Jack, but I'm not sure when he'll be able to get back to me."

She forced herself to stop and listen.

The line was quiet for too long and, in despair, Rosa wondered if the call had dropped, then a reply finally came.

"Of course, I'll watch her. I can be there in fifteen or so minutes."

"Thank you so much! Bless you!"

****

Sky stared at the phone, even after she'd disconnected. Her knuckles had whitened around it. With effort, she put it down and walked down the hall to her bedroom. She'd finished grading for the moment and had been relaxing in front of the TV watching an old Thin Man movie. Now, she stripped down from her pajamas and replaced them with jeans and a hoodie.

Was she really doing this?

Of course, she was. Despite the leaden dread inside, Jack's little girl needed her and she wouldn't let either one of them down. She felt for Rosa Cruz. Poor woman. What a horrible situation.

As she slipped her feet into previously tied sneakers, she decided to bring Avery home with her. The girl might think of it as a fun sleepover. They could even make a blanket fort and have snacks inside. Good thing she'd stopped at the store.

She'd call Jack once they were back at her place.

For a moment, she considered grabbing her raincoat, but dismissed it. She wouldn't be long. With her purse, keys, and phone in hand, she slipped out the side door to hurry toward her little SUV.

Chapter Thirty-Five

Avery could smell smoke mixed with a slightly sweet stench that made her want to gag, but she knew it wasn't real. It was just *him*.

He wanted her upset with Sky, but she didn't want to be. The burnt man said she was stubborn and it made him really mad, so she hid under her blanket. Even in the living room, he found her.

Rosa didn't notice. She kept pacing and looking out the front window. She already wore her rain slicker, and her purse was on the table right by the door.

Daddy had called back, speaking to Rosa and then to her for a few moments. She wanted to tell him, but the burnt man was a blobby shadow by the fireplace. Besides, Avery didn't think he'd believe her.

Terror speared through her when she heard the car outside beyond the steady thrumming of rain. She wanted to run to Sky to ask if they could just go back to her house, but the ghost was furious. Despite her push back, Avery could feel his anger seeping into her.

A moment later, the doorbell rang and Avery peeked out from under the blanket.

Skylar stepped inside, pushing back her hood. Damp blonde hair spilled over her shoulders as she spoke quietly with Rosa. Her face filled with compassion as she nodded, holding the older woman's hand in both of hers.

Rosa thanked her again, her voice breaking, before slipping out into the rain, pulling the door shut behind her.

Turning toward her, Sky smiled. Avery saw her shiver and her smile dimmed just a little. "Hey, Avi. What do you think about spending the night at my house? I can wait while you throw a few things together.

I'll call your dad when we get there."

All grown up. A real looker too. (Chuckle) I made that.

The thought wasn't hers and Avery frowned. The man remained by the fireplace, but his features began sharpening into horrifying detail. She didn't want to look at him and kept her gaze on Sky. Anger rose in her, hot and violent. She tried pushing it way. She tried really hard.

"I don't want to be mad at you," Avery whispered, her voice shaking.

"Mad at me?" Sky looked confused. "I don't understand, honey. Did I do something wrong?"

Avery shook her head as Skylar sat on the edge of the sofa next to her. "No, it's not me. It's *him.*"

"Him...?" Sky repeated, color washing from her face.

Feeling bad, Avery tried to stop the emotional torrent inside. She liked Sky and didn't want to hurt her. She wanted to hug her tight, but she was so very angry.

"If it weren't for you, he wouldn't be here! He said he was murdered!"

Skylar looked as if she'd been slapped, and Avery didn't understand why she'd said that or what was happening.

The burnt man laughed, the nasty sound echoing in her head. From the corner of her eye, she saw the man move. He seemed to rear up, grow larger, going up and over, like he was going to swallow her.

With a scream, Avery tumbled off the couch and ran. The little bit in her head that made sense told her to go, just get out. Without second guessing, she shoved open the glass slider and barreled out into the rain. She monkeyed over the fence and followed the path, tripping over a root once, pushing to her feet, and heading to the little tent. Maybe she'd be safe there.

****

Skylar felt as if she'd been punched in the stomach. She couldn't breathe and she was so cold she could barely flex her fingers. Leaning forward, she wrapped her arms around herself and tried to pull air into her lungs.

Him. Avery had said *him.*

Sky didn't have to ask who.

Memories slid past the block in her mind, oozing out like tendrils of darkness, threatening to strangle her.

The magazines. They'd been on the coffee table. The pictures were so pretty and she'd wanted to decorate the fort Stephen had built. With her red Crayola scissors, she'd cut some pictures out, just a few. Just the really nice ones. She'd taken them to tape them up inside the fort. Curling up on her blanket, she'd stared at them, wishing she could go into them. Maybe Mama and Stevie would come too.

He'd never find them then.

Did she fall asleep? She wasn't sure, but someone was yelling. There was the deep thunder of a voice. A big hand squeezed her arm, jerking her into awareness. His breath stunk of whiskey, and he spit as he yelled. She didn't cry when he hit her across the face, but she could taste blood in her mouth. Crying would show she was weak. She'd heard her brother say that. But she was weak. When he hit her again, she did cry. For some reason, that seemed to make him happy, but then he yanked her out of the fort. Something popped in her shoulder and, oh God, it hurt! She screamed as he dragged her up the path, jolting over ground roots, rocks digging into her legs and hips.

And then she was back in the house, drowning. Her throat burned, her nose ran, and she couldn't breathe…

Skylar came back, gasping and looking everywhere at once. Horror and panic twisted too tightly low in her stomach, bringing a wave of nausea.

The back slider door was open, the drapes billowing inward. Thunder rumbled a warning.

Oh, Jesus! Avery!

Despite feeling like her insides would soon shake to pieces, she shoved everything else aside and concentrated on Jack's little girl.

The past didn't matter, nor did the house and whatever resided within. She needed to make sure Avery was safe and get her away from here. Get them both away.

Darting outside, she paused to look around, blinking in the rain. Day evaporated quickly in the coming night and storm, but stubborn light remained in shades of gray, just enough for her to see.

At least for the moment.

The yard was cordoned off by a chain link fence, barely four feet tall. Beyond, the greenbelt pressed toward her, trees swishing, dark in warning. She then caught a glimpse of a narrow path.

She realized she knew it well.

Easily clearing the fence, she jogged toward the opening in the forest, years dropping before her. Not surprisingly, it was much more overgrown than it used to be and she had to crouch beneath low hanging branches and climb over a collection of fallen trees. When she entered the clearing, she stopped, staring. In the haze of waning light, she could see the drop off to the glen. Somewhere on the other side, Stephen's fort would have stood. They'd thought they'd be safe on the other side, until she wasn't.

Birds screamed from above and her gaze

wandered upward. All she saw were shadows, but she knew what they were. Death patiently watched and waited.

Fear kept her cold, but she pushed forward, listening and squinting. She wasn't sure how she knew the girl would be out here somewhere, she just knew without a doubt. In some sick sort of way, it made sense. *"Avery?"*

Looking one direction, then the other, she chose left, stepping along the tree line, straining her eyes and ears. "Avery, honey, where are you?"

Realization settled in and she crept toward the edge of the glen and stared downward, holding her breath. A flash flood wasn't outside the realm of possibility and the prospect of the little girl climbing down or falling into the gorge made her want to throw up. Relief rushed through her. No rising water. Not yet.

The rain shifted from a light but steady shower to big, fat, pelting drops. Lightning sent jagged shards through the sky, followed by the peal of thunder.

Thanking the universe, she pivoted, stopping when she caught a glimpse of pink toward the east end of the clearing. Stepping carefully, she found the little tent squeezed between two mature cedar trees and crouched before it.

"Avery?" She gentled her tone, not wanting the girl to think she was angry. She was scared enough.

A little voice responded, thick with sobs and snot. "I'm sorry. I'm really sorry. I didn't want to say those things."

With one hand, Sky moved aside the flap of the tent. "There's no reason to be sorry, sweetie. I know you didn't mean it. We should go, though. I don't think it's safe out here right now."

"I don't wanna go back in there!" Panic widened

the girl's eyes and her little body trembled. She squeezed herself into the back corner.

Pushing her sopping hair back from her face, Sky shook her head. "No, you're not going back inside. We're going to go over to Molly's, um, Ms. Achen's. You should be able to stay with her for a few minutes while I go back into your house to get my keys."

"You shouldn't go back in there."

"I didn't see anything, Avery." Even as she said it, she regretted it. The words felt foolish and patronizing.

"He sees *you*."

Chapter Thirty-Six

Jack couldn't settle.

Agitation crept under his skin, manifesting in a restlessness he couldn't quell no matter what he did. He'd gone out for happy hour with some colleagues and skipped most of the happy, choosing to return to the hotel and hit the gym. Exercise didn't help for once, despite following it up with some time in the sauna.

He'd tried to call the house, but there'd been no answer. It occurred to him that Sky may have taken Avery out and about, but when he tried her cell, it just went to voicemail. He'd left a message, but she'd hadn't gotten in touch yet. Of course, if they'd gone out to a movie, that would make sense.

Still...

Avery's voice had been off earlier. Sure, she'd said the right words, but his Daddy sense tingled. Then again, she could have been reacting to Rosa's distress.

Shit, he hated second guessing himself.

He paced his hotel room, while HBO presented an action flick with lots of explosions and quick cuts. Pausing, he switched it off, but the quiet made it worse. He turned the TV on again, changing the station to the Travel Channel. Maldives currently held the spotlight.

Crossing to the window, he stared out at the rain-drenched lights of Houston. Darkness had just coated the city. Despite the storm, he had a good view overlooking the convention center and the greenery below. He let the curtain drop.

Jack glanced down at his watch and 8:12 PM stared back at him.

It would take him a good three hours to get home, longer if there were any traffic incidents along I-10. He'd be surprised if that wasn't the case.

Without another thought, he walked into the bathroom to start gathering his toiletries.

Maybe he'd look foolish, but he'd be happy to do so as long as Avery and Skylar were okay.

Chapter Thirty-Seven

Skylar stared at the little girl for several long moments, the feeling of dread pervasive. "I'll just have to be fast then."

Avery returned her gaze, before nodding slowly. She didn't look convinced but seemed willing to give her the benefit of the doubt. On hands and knees, she crawled toward the front of the tent and into Sky's arms. Her body shook in spasms and Sky hugged her tightly, kissing the top of her head. "Let's go see Molly and Mr. Chuckles."

"Okay."

The storm had worsened, blending the glen and surrounding woods into a blotch of dripping watercolor. Lightning crisscrossed the sky, giving them the light of day for a second or two before it bled away, replaced by a loud clap of thunder.

"Take my hand. We need to stay together." The girl obeyed without comment, her grip closing in on painful.

They picked their way back toward the trail, moving slower than Sky would have liked, but risking a broken ankle or worse wasn't an option. Intense rain blurred everything and the once familiar seemed alien. They needed to be careful.

Above the din, birds screamed from the tops of the trees. They seemed to be competing with the prickly Texas weather. Another shudder quaked Sky to the bone, superstition a little too raw in the moment.

The trail would soon open up on their left. At that point, they'd only be a couple hundred yards from Jack's property. They'd be able to bypass the house and slip through the side yard next to the garage. She and Avery would be safe soon.

Lightning flashed again, bringing the aroma of ozone and a sharp crack across the night. From the corner of her eye, something rushed them. On instinct, she pushed Avery behind her just as it struck. Sky took a hard blow from the left. She was knocked down, wind rushing from her lungs, agony slicing through her head and shoulder. She was dimly aware of a loud snap from somewhere inside her own body.

Someone screamed and her sluggish, pain-filled mind had a moment to wonder who it was before fading away.

****

When Skyler shoved Avery, it had shocked a short cry from the girl. For a moment, confusion, hurt, and a tiny flame of anger had flickered, but they lost themselves in panic when the branch split and knocked the woman hard to the ground.

Avery crawled forward, tears mixing with rain against her face. "Sky?"

There was no response. In the light of another blast of lightning, she gasped. Blood coated half the woman's face, the other half rested in mud. One hand lay limp next to her head, the other arm stretched out at a weird angle. A large branch lay diagonal across her, but it had wedged against a tree trunk just opposite. As far as Avery could tell, there might be enough space to pull her out from under it. She didn't think she was strong enough though.

Afraid to touch her, afraid not to, she kneeled beside her and reached to push hair from Sky's face. Her eyes were closed and Avery couldn't tell if she was breathing or not.

"Please, Sky." She touched her right hand. "Sky?"

Nothing.

Swallowing, Avery looked around, considering what she should do. She didn't want to leave her, but she had no choice. Jumping to her feet, she hastened up the trail, hoping she wouldn't trip. She planned to get Mrs. Achen and, if she wasn't home, she'd be brave, suck it up, and go back into her house to call 9-1-1.

Sky was counting on her.

****

Molly arrived back home from her evening yoga class with water dripping off the ends of her braids. It always embarrassed her daughter when she put her hair in a Pippy Longstocking-esque style, so Molly was happy to establish it as a habit. It didn't seem to bother anyone else, or at least if it did, they had the good sense to keep their mouths shut.

After an hour of New Age music, Molly was ready for some Metallica and painting. She felt her creative juices stirring and needed to jump on it while she could. Pulling a stretched canvas from her pile in the corner, she secured it on the easel and considered. Would the image in her head be better represented by acrylic or watercolor? Or maybe gouache. It would have some elements of watercolor, but it wouldn't be quite as translucent.

Gouache, it was.

Digging in her taboret, she pulled out several tubes, putting them aside to look for one of her palettes. Humming along with the music because she avoided singing (she wouldn't do that to Mr. Chuckles), she almost didn't hear the knock.

Frowning, she looked at the clock. It wasn't even 8:30 PM, but she wasn't expecting anyone. Most of her yoga friends had gone out to imbibe in manufactured happiness at a local tavern. Molly hadn't been interested, so she'd just taken herself on home.

Mr. Chuckles had walked to the front door without a woof. He wagged his tail instead.

So, a friend.

Molly trusted Mr. Chuckles' judgment. She remembered how he didn't want to go next door a bit back. She'd respected his decision and had apologized to little Avery Langham with a 'maybe next time.'

Unlocking the deadbolt, she left the chain on when she opened the door to peer out. Just because Chuck had yet to be wrong didn't mean there couldn't be a first time. Molly wasn't a complete idiot.

Instead, Avery Langham stood under her porchlight, drenched, shaking, and crying.

"Dear Jesus, child! Hold on a sec!" She shut the door just long enough to unhook the chain, then pulled it open wide. When she reached to take her hand and pull her inside, the little girl backed away, shaking her head.

"Sky … Skylar's hurt! You have to help her. I'm not strong enough! Please!"

"What…?"

"Please! I don't want her to die!" The girl grabbed at her sleeve, her words melding together in harsh sobs. "She's alone in the woods!"

"Okay, darlin'. Hold on a sec." Molly opened the hall closet and grabbed one raincoat, then two. Reaching onto the top shelf, she felt around for a moment before her fingers curled around the handle of her flashlight. She pulled it down and leaned it against the wall. Draping one coat around the child, she slid into the other, shoving her phone and keys in one deep pocket.

"Stay, Chuck."

The dog whined but stayed in the entry as Molly shut the door behind them.

"Okay, Avery. Show me."

Chapter Thirty-Eight

Sky found herself lying face down at the edge of the glen. Pushing herself into a sitting position, she brushed dirt and rotten leaves off her sweatshirt.

Sunlight diffused through the clouds to cast an odd yellowish light. In the still moment awaiting thunderhead darkness, the air squeezed around her, thick and cloying. Surrounding creatures held their breaths, the decision to hide or go about their business contingent on a mass of building clouds. Confusion fogged her brain as she tried to piece together events leading her to this moment, gasping a moment later. "Avery!"

They'd been picking their way back out of the woods while the storm raged. Something fast and hard had hit her and then…

Avery wouldn't be here. Not here.

She touched her head with delicate fingers, but there was no pain. Her left shoulder seemed to be working okay as well. Trembling, she shoved to her feet, looking around. Her stomach twisted when she noticed Stephen's fort across the chasm.

Turning away, she looked for the trail leading to the neighborhood behind the greenbelt, but the trees seemed thicker, standing bare inches apart. They stood sentinel, keeping her inside.

High above, ravens hopped in the highest limbs, some circling above the clearing. They screamed their guttural cries, agitated or expectant. She could feel their intelligent, beady eyes affixed to her. Or maybe it was her imagination.

A deep, masculine chuckle bounced off the trees surrounding her and she swiveled, trying to look everywhere at once. Unsure of what else to do, Sky moved in the opposite direction, looking for a place to hide and some kind of weapon. She didn't want to be cornered, but she still preferred to have something at her back.

Whispers reached her, dim and muddled, but the voices sounded familiar. She stopped, tilting her head to listen, but they slid away before she could identify them. They were soon replaced with a man's echoing laugh.

"*What do you want?*" Not expecting an answer, she managed to keep her voice from shaking, even adding a layer of anger. Despite the terror she felt, she didn't want *him* to hear it.

"You didn't ask who, just what." It chuckled, the voice non-directional, the sound raspy and oddly wet. "Remember me, little Sky?"

She stumbled on some loose rocks and stopped. Leaning down, she grabbed one with heft and a jagged edge. As she walked, she held it down by her thigh, gripping it hard enough to make her hand hurt.

"You're not important enough to remember," Sky snapped back. Despite the fearful hammering of her heart, she didn't want to dissolve into a blubbering mess. She refused to.

Eyes darting, she continued searching for some kind of safe spot, somewhere she could see him coming. Tumbling back through time, she remembered when and how the habit had begun.

"As respectful as your brother, I see."

Sky pivoted quickly, swinging the rock as hard as she could, but a large, powerful hand caught her by the wrist, grinding the bones together. With a cry, she dropped her only weapon.

Gasping, she stared at the swollen, darkened fingers wrapped around her. A few nails were missing and the tips glistened. Its skin felt wet and oily against hers and a sweet, putrid smell rose around her.

Trembling, she slowly looked up into her nightmare. Less of a face and more of a Halloween mask stared down at her. One side of its head was smashed in, bloody chunks of scalp and hair dangling, the other side charred and barely recognizable as human. It smiled, one undamaged eye staring into hers. It was the same exact blue violet as hers. Sky couldn't speak, horror robbing her of voice and movement.

It leaned closer, its stench rushing at her face. "Not important enough, huh?"

With that, it let go with one hand and backhanded her with the other.

Sky tumbled backward over the edge of the embankment.

Chapter Thirty-Nine

Jack stopped at a truck stop for coffee and to check if anyone had gotten back to him.

Nothing.

He tried calling again, listening to Sky's voicemail greeting, leaving messages, knowing he sounded panicked but not caring.

Tension rolled through his shoulders, settling into a steady ache at the base of his skull as he strode into the convenience store. He bought a large travel cup of strong coffee and a protein bar to kindle his lagging energy levels. Ducking against the rain, he jogged back to his truck, his phone going off just as he swung into the driver's seat.

He didn't recognize the number, but picked it up with a curt greeting anyway, bracing himself.

"Jack?"

It took him a moment before the voice on the other end registered. "Ms. Achen?"

"Yes, it's Molly. First of all, I want you to know that Avery is fine. She's right here with me. You do need to come home though."

Relief weakened him, but the edge to her voice kept him on alert. "Actually, I'm on my way now. I couldn't get a hold of—wait, is Sky *okay*?"

Silence clung to the other end for a few long moments before she answered, her tone careful. "We're not sure yet. There was ... an accident. They're looking at her now. We're at Central Medical in a little waiting room on the third floor."

Jack felt like he was being strangled, his voice high and rough. "I'm still a couple hours out."

"I understand. We'll be here. Just be careful." She

hung up and he stared at his cell phone, questions and worry congealing into a painful mass in the pit of his stomach.

****

Molly disconnected, feeling old and tired for the first time ever.

From the moment she saw the young woman standing in front of the Langham house, she'd feared the worst. She just hadn't a clue as to how to voice her thoughts. Seriously. What was she supposed to say? Hey, kiddo, I kind of knew your daddy and he scared the hell out of me? Or, hey, Jack, I think your house has a lot of bad juju because of your girlfriend's dead father? How's that for a kicker?

Shaking her head, Molly gazed over at Avery. The girl was curled up in an uncomfortable waiting room chair, still wearing her borrowed coat. She was a little pale, but the kid had grit. She'd answered all questions from the medical staff, her voice quiet but steady. Now, she nibbled on a KitKat Molly had purchased for her and stared at a magazine.

With any luck, her dad would arrive soon.

Of course, Molly wasn't sure what she was going to tell him. The staff hadn't said much of anything to her because she wasn't related. She figured he was going to have the same damned problem. They said they weren't authorized to release information. Typical bullshit as far as Molly was concerned, but it was what it was. According to the nurses, they were attempting to get in touch with Skylar's emergency contact. But in the meantime, she, Jack, and Avery would all be in the dark.

All Molly could think was Skylar hadn't looked so good.

****

Chloe lay curled up next to him, one leg looped

over his, an arm around his torso. Her breaths came slow and heavy and he watched a few strands of her hair dance within them. Stephen didn't often feel content, but the moment was close. He considered it a small gift. Maybe it was because he planned on buying a ring when he got home. The word 'maybe' wasn't in his vocabulary regarding Chloe, at least not anymore. He wanted her in his bed every night from now on. He wanted kids with her, pets, a future. He'd even let her redecorate his house—he knew she was itching to, even if she didn't say it. Kissing the crown of her head, he caressed the soft skin of her back. She didn't stir, always having been a deep sleeper.

There was a little relief there too, he had to admit. He wanted to come clean now, even needed to. Sky deserved to know everything. Both Benny and Chloe assured him that she'd forgive him. He could only hope they were right. And Mama deserved to come home. He refused to think she wouldn't be approved for parole, his mind's eye filled with images of driving down to pick her up. It would be tough on her, but he'd be there. And so would Sky.

Perhaps things really would be okay.

When the phone on his nightstand began buzzing, he just stared at it and Chloe continued sleeping in his arms, undisturbed.

It was a little after 10:00 PM. It could be Sky or Benny.

Craning his neck, he frowned. His didn't recognize the number popping up.

When something cold dropped in his belly, he reached over, fumbling for it, knocking it off the nightstand. "Shit!"

Chloe snorted in her sleep and rolled away from him, going quiet again at the same time the phone stopped ringing.

Gritting his teeth, Stephen pushed the sheets back and eased out of bed. He reached for his boxer shorts and yanked them on before swooping the phone off the carpet and padding out to the living room.

They'd left the lamp next to the couch glowing, but he didn't bother to sit. He paced instead, wanting a cigarette before he called the number back, calling it first anyway.

The woman who answered the phone redirected his call to a nurse's station and after identifying himself, Steve listened to someone tell him a lot of nothing about his little sister. The only thing clear was that he'd be pulling in a favor from an acquaintance and flying tonight, not driving down tomorrow.

Chapter Forty

The biting smell of alcohol and disinfectant attacked his sinuses when Jack stepped from the elevator. He took a left and followed signs toward the 3rd floor waiting room, his footsteps muted by industrial carpeting, his movements numb, robotic.

Ominous double doors waited before him, the waiting room filling an alcove just to his right. About a dozen chairs lined the wall and formed a row down the center, while a television anchored in a corner by the ceiling spread its rancor by talking heads and subtitles.

Avery leapt at him and he lifted her, holding her close.

Molly approached him, face wan, pigtails drooping. Her pant legs and shoes were caked with dirt. For the first time since they'd met, she looked elderly. It shook him more than he cared to admit.

"They haven't really told us anything because we're not kin." Her voice held the bite of anger. "They're waiting for her emergency contact."

Jack nodded, letting Avery slide to her feet. She huddled against him and he kept an arm around her. When he spoke, his voice shook. "What happened?"

Molly and Avery looked at one another for a couple moments before the woman sighed. "It seems a large branch split in the storm and walloped Skylar. Avery came to find me and we called 9-1-1."

Staring at them, Jack tried to unravel the words and make sense of what she told him. He couldn't. "I don't understand. Why was she out in the storm?"

"It was my fault, Daddy." Avery gazed up at him, her eyes full. "She came to find me. We were walking back when the storm got really bad. Sky pushed me out of the way, so it hit her instead."

"It wasn't her fault. The kiddo was spooked," Molly said, her tone firm.

Jack started to question, shutting his mouth when he heard rushed footsteps from the elevator.

A dark-haired man walked toward the double doors, not even looking their way. He wore a mask of tension, eyes shadowed. He reached out to push through, stopping when Molly spoke.

"Stephen Donoghue?"

The man paused, frowning. He cut Molly a questioning look, then met Jack's gaze for a moment before nodding. Without a word, he pushed through to approach the nurses' station on the other side.

She sighed under Jack's puzzled scrutiny and found her seat. "Maybe I should start at the beginning."

He sat opposite her, Avery sitting beside him, her hand snug in his. "Please. I feel completely out of the loop here."

"Just know that I've lived in my house a very long time. I raised my daughter there and grew older with my husband there. He passed away a few years back, but I love my house. As much as my kid bitches about me living alone down here, I'm not leaving. At least, I won't while my brain is still doing its job. Sorry, I think I just digressed." She stared beyond him for a moment before returning her gaze his way. "So, let me get back on track. Over thirty-five years ago, this young couple moved in next door to me. She was the prettiest little thing with long black hair and a sweet smile. He was movie star handsome—blond with the most *vibrant blue eyes*. They looked like they could walk down the red carpet together, you know what I mean?"

Jack shifted, his mouth drooping a little. Something sick festered inside and he swallowed.

"We all know looks can be damned deceptive though, huh? They pretty much kept to themselves, other than a polite wave or a little small talk. When I managed to talk to her, she always seemed skittish, like she was afraid to be seen chatting with a neighbor. They soon had a baby boy. As he got bigger, I remember a good-looking but really serious kid who kept to himself. And then they had a little girl—a beautiful child with eyes like her father."

"My husband and I liked to take our daughter and travel. We considered it the best education, so I wasn't always there, but enough to suspect things weren't a fairytale for that young woman. One time, she and I happened to be picking up our mail at the same time. She had one hell of a shiner. Even with makeup, it was a doozy."

"Christ," Jack muttered, the sickness blending with anger.

Molly nodded and looked away for a moment. When she met his gaze, her eyes held a sheen of tears. "I told her I'd help her and her children get away from him. I even offered to give her some money and drive them to a shelter or wherever she wanted to go. I would even get them on a bus, if that's what she wanted. But she wouldn't do it. She told me thank you, but keep out of it, intimating that *I* could get hurt. To be honest, I ignored her and called the police, but nothing came out of it."

"One day I was raking the front yard and the woman's husband approached me. He tried to charm me with a megawatt preacher-type smile, but you know what? Those gorgeous eyes of his were dead, cold, like something sinister was staring out from behind them. Like a devil."

Jack thought of Skylar's eyes. They were warm and compassionate, often glinting with humor. They were also haunted. With growing dread, he suddenly understood why.

"He 'thanked me for my concern,' but told me his wife was mentally unstable, that she'd go off her meds and sometimes hurt herself. I knew he was full of sh—" She glanced at Avery. "Crap. But he also, well, got a little too close, saying something to the effect that people can be injured or killed very easily, that we're a vulnerable species as a whole. He also mentioned that bad things can happen to anyone, regardless of their age."

Molly looked Jack in the eye. "Denise, my *daughter*, was twelve at the time. She went to school with Stephen. So, I backed off. I won't even try to tell you he didn't scare me, because he sure as heck did."

"So, I avoided them the best that I could. I was really PO'd, but I was frightened even more. The last time I saw any of them, it was just the kids. The little girl was playing in the front yard with this dirty, stuffed dog. Her brother had climbed the big tree on the property and was keeping watch, from what I could see. My family and I left to go up to Austin. We were spending the day up there and then going to the theater. I remember my Denise being so excited. We got home late that night, but couldn't even get near our house. The street was blocked off by the police and the fire department."

Molly quieted then, staring down at her hands.

He could see them shaking. "What happened, Molly?" Jack didn't want to know, but felt he needed to.

She shook her head. "I don't know much. I heard the children were sent away. I found out *he* was dead and heard rumors that that poor abused woman was arrested. I never found out anything beyond that. Truthfully, at that point, I wasn't sure I even wanted to know."

Jack dropped his head into one hand, an

overwhelming sense of horror and loss rippling through him. His eyes stung.

"Our house was *their* house, Daddy," Avery said, her voice soft. "That's why Sky tried to stay away. It was bad for her."

Chapter Forty-One

Sky tumbled down the embankment, splashing into a winded sprawl half in and half out of the shallow creek cutting through the center of the chasm. Frigid, the water soaked the left side of her body and she crawled from it, struggling to gain her breath.

John Patrick stood fifteen feet above her, his wet sounding chuckle resonating through the clearing. "You need to show some respect, little Sky."

He hit her mother across the face and she banged her head against the door. She slid down to the floor, crying. Sky tried to put herself between them, but he'd swatted her away like she was nothing.

Anger shoved away fear. Pushing to her feet, she glared up at him. She wanted to scream that he didn't deserve any respect, that the only thing he deserved was his own cozy little place in hell, but she thought better of it. Whether this was a dream world or a vivid hallucination, it was abundantly clear she was stuck in here with him. Taunting him would only succeed in pissing him off. It would also make him anticipate more fight from her.

Sky bit back her words. Instead, she made her way several yards upstream and crossed the creek using the weathered two by four Stephen had wedged there years ago. She clawed her way up the other side of the ravine, figuring she could try to keep that expanse between them.

"So, you're wondering what I want, huh?"

His rumble was right behind her. Startled, she jerked around and backed away. He didn't move forward, just stood watching with his one good eye. Repulsive and terrifying, Sky hated looking at him, but for whatever reason, he held a sick fascination and she couldn't look away.

"To be honest, you're not the preferred one, but you *were* convenient. I could feel you the moment you stepped back into the house, like you woke me after a really long sleep. Rip Van Winkle but with burns and blood instead of a long beard."

"*Right* one…?"

The man-thing rested on a stump, his tone initially conversational, turned acid-laced. "Yeah. You weren't a bad kid, for the most part. A little whiny maybe, but that's probably a girl thing. Your brother, on the other hand, well, he's a different story."

Skylar waited, nauseated and shaking with rage and fear.

"Always watching and judging me. The little fucker hardly spoke. Even when I had to beat his ass, he didn't make a sound. Of course, your stupid mother made excuses, claiming her own father's stoicism or some such Indian shit and how he was just like him, yadda, yadda, yadda."

Mawmaw had always said how much Stephen was like the grandfather they'd never known. Their mother hadn't lied.

"I admit I did lose control that night." He shrugged but then leaned forward, fixing her with a steely glare from his eye. "It doesn't excuse what he did!"

After he'd dragged her back to the house, Mama had rushed forward to help her, but he'd shoved her away, telling her he'd take care of his daughter just fine thank-you-very-much—she'd feel better very soon. Sky had been screaming and crying, her arm hurt so much. Then he was making her drink something. It was vile and burning. She didn't want it and tried pushing it away. So much stronger, he made her drink more. She gagged and spit, but he was relentless. When she tried to seal her lips, he'd held her nose, forcing her to take a breath. He made her drink more. Sky swallowed, coughed, even threw up a little. She couldn't breathe. Then he dropped her. A strong young voice cut through the fog of Skylar's brain. "Leave her alone, you son of a bitch!"

"The thing is, he's not here." The grisly face had turned away for a moment, but swung back toward her. "But, he will be soon. You just need to do that trick you used to do."

Confused, Sky shook her head. "I don't know what you're talking about."

"Eh, you may not remember, but it doesn't matter." He grinned and she shuddered. "You'll do it automatically. You'll bring him in here just like you used to."

"You want him here so you can *kill* him?"

"No, actually I can't touch him. You know how it is when you're asleep. If you dream you're about to die, you just—" John Patrick snapped his fingers, more of a click when the skin sloughed off the tips and bones peeked out. He stared at it. "Huh. Well, you just wake up, right?"

Skylar didn't respond. She was staring at his fingers.

"You're not listening!" The sudden noise made the ravens above squawk in displeasure and Sky shrank away.

When he saw he had her attention again, he continued, back to relaxed and chatty. "So, see? I can't hurt him. He's immune to me, but … unfortunately for you, little Sky, you're in a bit of a pickle out there. You're injured and that makes you vulnerable. I could sense you were here before. Hard to explain. I just knew.

'Course I didn't have that much effect on you, not then at least. Other than making you damned uncomfortable, I mean. Now things have *changed*." He grinned his ghastly grin and waved an arm. "This is my turf. You die in here, you die out there."

Sky stared at him, her heart thudding even faster.

"But, when he gets here, he'll see me do it. And he'll know, without any doubt, that your death will be *his* fault."

"Why would you do this to your own children?" She could barely form the words.

"Actually, it didn't start out as personal. You were just a couple of tools, but everything changed that night. Be sure to ask your big brother that question before you die."

Chapter Forty-Two

Stephen left Skylar's hospital room feeling numb.

The doctor had been upfront about her injuries. She'd suffered a broken shoulder, but it wasn't displaced, so it should heal without surgery. Of course, there were numerous cuts and abrasions, but all of it was, more or less, superficial. The real concern was the fact that she'd been unconscious over four hours. They said there was reaction to pain stimulus, which was good, according to some scale they measured by, so they suspected a brain contusion or concussion. She should wake up on her own, but there was no way to say when. Brain injuries were hard to predict. He was basically told that they needed to wait and see.

He stepped out through the double doors and looked over at the small group huddled in the waiting area. The other man rose to face him and Stephen had little doubt this was the guy his sister was falling for. Jack Langham stood several inches taller than him and he also looked like he was going to puke.

Stephen held out a hand, which the other man clasped in tense greeting. "Jack Langham? I'm Stephen, Skylar's brother."

"Stephen." The man nodded.

He looked at the old woman, wondering who the hell she was and how she knew him. He dismissed the curiosity, at least until a later time. It didn't matter right now.

Turning back to Jack, he plowed forward, trying to keep his voice even. "Sky has a broken shoulder, numerous cuts and bruises, but the main issue is she hasn't regained consciousness yet. They're saying possible brain contusion or concussion. Or something like that."

"She's *comatose*?"

"Basically, yeah. Right now, they're adopting the whole 'wait and see approach.' I guess there is some response, which they say is good of course, but they can't predict when she might awaken. It could be … anytime."

Implications sunk in and Stephen tried to steel himself, but he couldn't quite do it like he used to. The gradations of life had begun to mean much more.

"So, can anyone tell me what happened to my sister?" He struggled to keep any anger or accusation out of his voice.

"I think we were just getting to that." Jack glanced at the woman, before returning his gaze. "But, it would seem I may have purchased your childhood home."

Stephen nodded. Even though Sky had told him as much, the knowledge still made his head spin.

The old woman stepped toward him. "I know you don't remember me, but I lived next door to you. And I still live next door to that house."

He looked from one to the other. "For years, I'd thought it burned to the ground. Sky told me differently several days ago. It's hard to even fathom."

"I bet. The damage was actually just confined to one area of the house. It was rebuilt and changed, tweaked, whatever, over the years. A year or so ago, I noticed a contractor restoring it again and when I returned home after visiting my daughter and her family, Jack and Avery lived there."

"What are the odds?" Stephen shook his head, implications cutting deep. "I'm sorry. That's unfortunate, but right now I honestly don't care. What I need is to know what happened to Sky. Why the hell is she here?"

To his surprise, the little girl answered, her voice soft and wavering. "The burnt man lives in my house. He tried to control me by scaring me. He wanted me angry with Sky. I don't know why, but I didn't want to be. I like her too much. She couldn't see him, neither could Dad and Rosa, but *I* could. I ran outside to get away from him. There's a trail behind my house—I set up my tent out there by that little canyon. She came out to find me despite the rain. We were just going to go back to her house until Daddy got home, but this big branch broke in the storm. It fell down toward us. Sky pushed me away so I didn't get hit. It hit her instead. I'm so sorry, Sky's brother!"

Her voice shook apart and she started crying.

Her father immediately sat down and gathered her into his lap, whispering calming words to her.

Frowning, he glanced at Jack. The man looked back, gaze steady.

Realization and shock twisted together low in his belly, the pain of his ulcer erupting into a quick blaze.

It really was true. *John Patrick* had Sky. After all these years, some part of the fucker was still around. He thought of those books he'd found years before. Had whatever the man been into preserved him in some way? *The girl said he was burned, so he couldn't be that strong still, could he?*

The girl was still crying and Stephen crouched down next to her. "This is *not* your fault."

She'd been pressing her face into her dad's neck, but hesitantly turned to look at him. His heart broke at the poor kid's expression. "It's not?"

"No. It's mine." He straightened, unsure what to do. Maybe he should go to that house? Would that even do anything? Would the asshole sense him or whatever?

Apparently, he'd sensed Sky.

Another voice, a far more practical one, reminded him that this could all be a coincidence. Sky could just have been injured in a freak accident, and there was nothing supernatural or remarkable about it. The kid could just have one hell of an imagination. His little sister could just wake up when she was ready.

No, that wasn't it. He'd expected something since Sky returned here. Chloe had even voiced concern after learning more about his past. Maybe everything went full circle for a reason. Stephen needed to end what he thought he'd finished almost a quarter of a century ago. The difference being, he was no longer a twelve-year-old kid. And Skylar wasn't six. He wondered if that phantasm son of bitch had even considered that. Probably not.

"I think maybe you should see Sky. Talk to her. Keep talking to her." He met Jack Langham's eyes. "She needs to hear your voice."

"I want to see her, but they've been pretty clear about hospital regulations." The quiet plea in the man's voice told Stephen that his sister's feelings were most likely reciprocated. Relief and sadness twisted together. They didn't blend well.

"I want to see her too." Little Avery Langham looked up at him from a dirty, tear-streaked face.

Stephen addressed the girl first. "I know Skylar would love you to visit, but unless you can grow a couple feet in the next minute, they won't buy that you're eighteen. I'm sorry, honey."

Turning, he studied Jack for a moment, considering. "This is going to sound nuts, but before I try to waggle you in there, I want permission to visit that … *your* … house. Is that okay?"

"Um … yeah. Of course." He fished in his

pocket, pulled out his house keys, and handed them over. A tiny Snoopy hung on the keyring and Stephen almost smiled. Probably a gift from the kid.

"Why don't I take Avery home with me? The poor girl's ready to drop. She can curl up in my guest room. Stephen can ride along with me, so he can do what he feels he needs to," Molly offered. Her tone was less of an offer and more of an order.

After a long moment's hesitation, Jack nodded.

"Okay, Avi. I want you to go with Ms. Achen." Even as the little girl shook her head, he hugged her and kissed her forehead. "You'll be fine, baby."

He released her to Molly, who took the girl's hand. "I'll see you soon."

Langham followed Stephen through the double doors. In step, they approached the nurse's station and he addressed the first nurse. "This is my sister's fiancé, Jack Langham. He needs to see her."

"Of course. I didn't realize." The nurse nodded, apology and compassion schooled into her features.

A subtle widening of the eyes showed Langham's surprise, but he gave no sign otherwise.

"Keep talking to her, okay? Keep her with us." Stephen wasn't positive it would help, but his instincts told him it was the right thing.

Jack nodded, pausing long enough to mouth 'thank you,' when the nurse indicated he should follow.

Stephen gazed toward the room where his sister was, before dropping his eyes to his feet. He concentrated on his breathing so he wouldn't picture his baby sister lying comatose and helpless. He wasn't even sure what he could do, but he needed to do *something*.

He returned to the waiting room to catch a ride.

His past was running to catch up with him.

Chapter Forty-Three

When Molly pulled her little Subaru up next to her travel van, Stephen soaked in her home, then the one next door. The neighborhood had always been dark and that hadn't changed, but he could see enough to know it was the street where he'd spent the worst years of his life.

Hands clammy, he rubbed them against his jeans. It pissed him off to realize he felt fear. It wasn't fear of loss this time, it was a deep, primal fear of the unknown, of the layers he suspected existed on the edge of death and just beyond.

The old woman had given him her phone number, as well as Jack Langham's, and now turned toward him. "Okay, you watch your ass in there, kid."

"Will do. By the way, I think I do remember you now. Your daughter is … Deena, right?"

"Denise." She seemed pleased he remembered them.

"She was cute. Had a birth mark right here." He pointed just under his ear.

Molly laughed. "She did and she didn't think you knew she existed."

"I did notice her. I just couldn't pay much attention." Sadness touched his words and he gave her a small smile. With that, he opened the door and started climbing out, stopping when Avery spoke from the back seat. He'd thought she was asleep.

"Be careful, Mr. Stephen. Please help Sky. I'm pretty sure my dad loves her."

His chest constricted and he couldn't look at either one of them. "I'll do my best."

Without looking back, he shut the door and

crossed the wet lawn toward his childhood home. The grass made sucking sounds as he stepped through it, his eyes fixed on the craftsman before him. Someone had left the porch light on and he could get an idea how aesthetically pleasant the house likely was. It was in much better shape now. New paint—a blue or turquoise color from what he could see, instead of the pale yellow it'd been before. There was nothing peeling, no missing shutters, no sagging first step going up to the front patio. The yard was meticulous, the old elm in front even bigger, of course, but trimmed so it didn't brush the roof of the house.

Pulling in a breath, he fetched the keys from his front pocket and let himself inside.

Polished wood floors had replaced old beige wall to wall carpet. A large throw rug was spread in the front room, resting beneath a comfortable looking sectional. There was a distressed oak coffee table and a big screen TV Stephen couldn't help but approve of. The fireplace was lined in rock instead of brick, just next to a couple of large bookshelves. Darkness pressed against the glass slider and he knew where it led.

He didn't smell anything burning, only the aroma of lemon Pledge and Windex.

Almost reverent, he checked each room, noting Sky's old room was now Avery's and his had been converted to an office. Of course, his parents' room was now Jack's, but it was shaped a little different, bigger, more of a rectangle than a square. The master bath was also larger with a separate tub and shower. It used to be just a combination. He wandered into the kitchen. Once again, it was different, much more modern. Opening the small door off the fridge, he peered up the narrow stairs, breathing deep. No smell of smoke. Not that he expected it in that tiny attic space. As far as he remembered, the old man never bothered to go up there.

"Okay, fucker. I'm home." Stephen spoke loudly, unsure what he should expect. According to the little girl, no one else saw the burnt man.

Nothing.

Unsure what to do, he pulled out a chair and settled at the kitchen table. He tapped his fingers against the wood, gaze darting around. "Hey, asshole! Still bullying just women and children, I hear. I always wondered what it would be like if you pissed the wrong guy off. Someone bigger, nastier, and meaner than your pathetic ass."

Stephen got up again, roaming. He stopped before the glass slider and peered into darkness. He flipped the switch on the wall and weak light from the back porch didn't reach past the jungle gym. The woods and the glen crouched beyond that child's toy, waiting.

Switching on the flashlight app on his phone, he opened the door and stepped out. The rain had stopped, but humidity hung in the cool air to dampen his skin. By memory, he leapt over the fence, looking for the trail. Despite the dense foliage, he found it, following carefully, keeping an eye where he stepped. He had to climb over a fallen tree and duck under another, but he reached the clearing and the glen. Above, clouds decided to part and watery light from the moon glowed down over him.

Other than the occasional movement from nocturnal creatures, he didn't hear anything. He looked up toward the tree tops, but the ravens were nowhere to be seen. Maybe that was a good thing. No, as long as Sky lay unconscious in a hospital room, nothing was a good thing.

He peeked in the ravine, noting the storm water cutting through the glen. No way to cross that right now, at least not safely. If he wanted to get to the other side, he'd have to take the long way. But he didn't see the point. It occurred to him that this wasn't where he needed to be.

Pivoting around, he picked his way back to the house, turning off the flashlight and wiping his feet on the doormat. Stephen had been up over twenty hours and exhaustion settled deep into his muscles and bones. He figured he'd fall asleep pretty quickly. He also suspected Skylar would then take it from there.

Pulling off his boots, he stretched out on the long side of the sectional, tucking a throw pillow behind his head. Staring up at the ceiling, he listened to the quiet of the house. A quiet that hadn't existed when he'd lived in it.

Stephen closed his eyes and let his mind drift.

****

John Patrick tilted his head back and closed his good eye. He seemed to be listening or perhaps tapping into some sense he alone possessed.

While he was distracted, Sky turned to search for a weapon. She'd have to be mindful not to alert him. If she saw anything, anything at all, she'd need to stay subdued and wait for her chance. The man, *the thing*, was disintegrating and she refused to believe he was invulnerable.

Off to her right, she thought she saw a branch poking from beneath a pile of dead leaves. It was only a couple yards away. She wondered what her odds were. For a rotting piece of meat, he was disturbingly strong and fast. It didn't matter though. She had little to lose.

He opened his eye and looked at her. Without that awful grin, she couldn't tell any expression, the tiny muscles promoting any subtlety long gone. "Gonna be show time soon, little Sky. You need to get with the program."

"I still don't know what you're talking about."
She backed a couple steps closer to that branch and just
out of arm's reach of the ghost or whatever the hell he
was. Her voice shook and she despised being afraid.

A long, rattling sigh escaped him and the stench
of rot made her stomach spasm. "You did it when you
were scared. That's what your mama said. You'd bring
her into your dreams. She said you brought Stevie in
too."

"I don't remember anything like that." As the
words passed her lips, her mind flickered to a recent
dream, one where Jack appeared, confused and
wondering what the hell the John Patrick monster was. It
didn't mean anything though. Just because she dreamed
about him didn't mean he was actually there. Her father-
thing had long ago slipped into insanity.

John Patrick rose to his feet, standing above her,
his charred and rotting face in full sunlight. A few
maggots dropped from a hole just below his jawline.
"You need to be scared though. Terrified even. Are you,
little Sky? Are you scared yet?"

Chapter Forty-Four

Jack hated hospitals. He remembered identifying Nikki and feeling like he'd become an instant husk. He could breathe, eat, and walk, sure, but everything that made him, *him*, had vanished into nothingness. It even overshadowed Avery's hospital birth. Profound guilt had twined with sadness when he'd come to that realization.

It had taken him a long time to crawl out of that perpetual state of numbness. He finally brought himself to move forward to not only care about another woman, but to actually love her. And now here he was again.

But Sky is not dead.

Yet.

Gritting his teeth, he shook his head. No. That wasn't going to happen. That couldn't happen. Law of averages and that.

He wished he could be as sure as the adamant voice in his head.

The nurse led him to the room farthest from the double doors. A single chair was set up next to the hospital bed. The window on the other side obscured the night sky with cheap blinds.

"Be mindful that you may see her eyes move, possibly even open. Sometimes someone in this situation will even speak nonsense. Both aren't uncommon for patients with head injuries. However, if she actually seems to respond to you, please hit the call button."

Jack just nodded and she left him there, walking away on crepe soled shoes.

He lowered himself into the uncomfortable chair and let his gaze fall to Sky's face for the first time since entering the room.

Pale, her flesh almost matched the pillow case,

making the deep purple bruising by her left eye and temple all the more startling. Near her hairline, several butterfly bandages held a long laceration together. Betadine, blood, and mud stained her golden locks.

She was hooked up to several monitors that beeped steadily within the hush of the room. Her breathing seemed a little fast, but at least it was regular. Jack didn't see any eye activity and he wasn't sure if he was relieved or disappointed.

With a gentle touch, he took her hand in his, wincing at how cold it felt. He placed his other hand over the top of hers in an attempt to warm it.

He couldn't help but wonder what Skylar's brother intended to do. Jack had already been knocked sideways and back, considered the kind of past his house held, but the whole supernatural element … well, he wasn't sure what to think. But now he knew the reason why she tried to pull away from him.

Kissing her cold hand, he pressed it to his cheek and just started talking about the first thing that came to mind.

****

Sky took another step back, gaze darting away from the thing before her but finding its way back because she didn't want him out of her sight.

He laughed, wet and phlegmy, moving closer.

She matched the difference in the other direction, in some kind of macabre dance. The thought made her want to giggle and that worried her a little. Clenching her jaw, she stepped back again.

"How do you have any control … out there?" She suspected he enjoyed hearing himself speak, so asking questions seemed a reasonable distraction until she could figure out what she should do.

"It's limited. I know *you* were affected by me. I

could sense it, but it's because we're blood. For most everyone else, I can only ingratiate myself a little if someone's asleep." He laughed. "Ask your boyfriend about it. I encouraged him to have one hell of a wicked nightmare. Of course, he didn't see beyond a bad dream. Kids are different though. Easier to shape, easier to manipulate. Everyone knows they're more open to unnatural occurrences than adults are."

"Is that what you are? An unnatural occurrence?" It came out with more venom than she intended.

His one eye narrowed and he leaned toward her. "Maybe to the blind and ignorant, but in the larger scheme? No. I am where I need to be. After I make what most would consider the ultimate sacrifice, I'll be restored and I'll move to the next realm. My brethren are waiting for me there."

"Your … *brethren*?"

"Others who studied, sacrificed, believed as I did. We will be rewarded beyond the curtain."

Oh, God. He's a zealot. Sky fought back another giggle, wondering if her own sanity was beginning to stretch out of shape.

A whisper reached her ears and she tilted her head ever so slightly. A gentle baritone. She couldn't quite distinguish all the words, just bits and pieces, but she knew that voice. The giggle transitioned into a borderline sob, but she held it back.

Jack was speaking to her. His tone was soothing, encouraging, loving. She had a quick, blurry image of him sitting by her bedside, holding her hand. She could even feel his warm flesh against hers. He leaned closer and his features came into focus enough to see them slide from worry to hope. His eyes shone. Then he was gone again.

"No, you fucking don't!" The sudden blow

knocked her backward into some tall weeds. She tasted blood in her mouth. "You are not going anywhere, little Sky!"

Ravens began screaming from above them, and somewhere beyond the trees, she heard a shout that might have been her name. A thin beam of excitement sliced through her, only to be trampled by its meaning. Her time was almost up.

The burnt man also heard it. His second of anger evaporated and he smiled down at her. "Time to start screaming, little Sky. The louder and more painful, the better. Bring him this way."

Sky rolled onto her side to push herself into a crouch, the tree branch less than a foot away from her hands.

The memories had come back, at least as many as she was capable of embracing, considered how young she'd been. She recalled shouting, shoving, hitting, her mother crying too many times. It was an amalgamation of snippets from a childhood that should never have been. *That* night, she'd been in so much pain and the bastard thought he was being funny by pouring liquor down her throat. He bragged that "he was going to make her feel better." Mama jumped on his back, but he knocked her off. Then Stephen was behind him. Sky had barely been conscious by that time, but she remembered a boy's face hardened with such anger and loathing. She didn't remember anything else until Stephen was waking her up and leading her from the house late that night.

"Come on, little Sky. Scream for me!" His eye glittered as he sang the last three words in a mocking falsetto. When he reached for her, she grabbed the branch and leaped up from a crouch, swinging it upward like a Louisville Slugger. It was heavier than she thought, but she was in good shape, so it didn't impede her. Panic, desperation, and a steady growing fury fueled her attack.

It connected just under the right side of his chin with solid crack, but she didn't know if it was the branch or his jawbone that made the sound. The man roared like a bear and Sky was satisfied to hear pain in the sound. She was right. He wasn't invulnerable.

She lashed out with it again, a solid blow to what was left of one ear.

"You bitch!" He caught the branch and pulled her forward and off balance. Stumbling, she tried to shift her wait to compensate, but he caught her by the throat. Reaching up, she grabbed at his hand, feeling some of his flesh slide off.

"C'mon, you little fucker! Baby sis needs her big brother!" John Patrick bellowed, his head lifting, eye rolling around.

He began squeezing.

Chapter Forty-Five

Holding his breath, Jack pulled his chair closer. He touched her cheek. "Sky?"

He could have sworn he saw awareness in those beautiful eyes for a moment. The heavy weight of disappointment settled over him when they slid shut again.

They'd said she might open her eyes, but it didn't mean she was coming back. Sometimes it was just a reflex from deep inside. Swallowing, he continued holding her hand and went on with his river-rafting-gone-to-shit story.

****

Stephen didn't awaken in the glen this time. He'd opened his eyes to find himself next to a moss-covered tree on the trail. He called out for Sky, hushing a second later, regretting the impulse.

He wanted to run, but held himself to a fast but careful walk. He didn't want to risk injuring himself, even if he was in a dream. There was no way of knowing if it would contribute to Skylar's fate.

Just before he reached the glen, he heard a distorted version of a voice he hadn't heard since he was twelve. It sounded as if John Patrick had gargled with acid, but the mocking rage behind it was too familiar. Ice crystals seemed to form in his blood even as perspiration covered his forehead and dampened his armpits. Gritting his teeth, he stepped out into the clearing. He approached the edge of the canyon, fear and dismay wedging themselves deep into his heart. The normal benign trickle of water at the bottom had become a dream world torrent. The 2x4 they'd always used to traverse the stream had disappeared.

Across the chasm, a melting husk of a man, a nightmare *thing*, held his sister by the throat. It turned its head to look at him and grinned. "Welcome home, *Stevie*."

Acid bubbled up from his stomach and he swallowed back bile. John Patrick had probably turned the creek into a river on purpose, so Stephen would be powerless to help Sky.

Stephen knew he wouldn't have enough time to cross farther north where the water disappeared underground. She'd already be dead by then.

****

Jack jumped to his feet when Skylar started gasping, lips tinting blue. He smacked the call button, but rushed to the entrance of the room in panic.

"She can't breathe!" The words didn't sound loud enough, caught somewhere between his diaphragm and his lips.

It didn't matter.

Before he could blink, a rush of medical personnel converged in the small space, shoving him out into the hallway. Helpless, he watched through the glass partition, not noticing the wetness against his cheeks.

****

Her father-thing had turned its gaze to watch Stephen emerge from the woods, but his grip didn't ease.

The pressure on her throat cut off her oxygen and she flailed at him. His skin sloughed off when she tried to pry his hand free, leaving her with nothing to grab onto. Black spots pushed in from her periphery and she fought harder, slamming her foot onto his instep and kicking his shin. For a moment, her shoe got stuck, as if his bones were turning to mush and she stumbled backward. Taken off balance, he fell forward, catching himself but loosening his hold. Sky sucked in a couple gulps of air, coughing when her shocked lungs reacted. When she turned to run, he grabbed her hair and pulled her back into him, his chest making a squishing sound at impact.

He held her tightly, one hand digging into her upper arm, the other gripping just under her chin. Keeping her close, he shifted them to face the figure on the other side.

"You always were a fucking coward." Although he didn't raise his voice, Stephen's words found their way across the glen with ease.

Skylar felt the rumble as the thing behind her growled. "You have no idea what you're dealing with. You never did. You may have killed me out there, but I'm still here."

"And not looking so good either."

Shock threaded through every nerve in Sky's body. *Avery had told her the burnt man said he'd been murdered.*

"Just temporary, I assure you." He tightened his grip under her chin. "You hear that, little Sky? He doesn't even deny it. Came into my bedroom in the middle of the night and bashed my head in with that baseball bat of his. I was asleep, so who's really the coward?"

Trying to block out their words, she jabbed backward with her elbow, sickened by the spongy feel as it connected with his midsection. It had little effect. He only tightened his hold.

"Are you ready to watch her die, you little shit?"

Across the way, Stephen stood still, his hands balled at his sides. "John Patrick! Why don't you come over here and take me on instead? Oh, that's right, silly me, you only pick on women and children."

The thing tensed before chuckling. "Nah, this will

hurt more. You'll spend the rest of your life knowing your sister's death was entirely on you."

John Patrick turned her to face him, his fetid breath flowing over her. Behind her, she heard Stephen call out, his voice pleading.

"This is *your* dream, Skylar. He's dead. He's nothing." Almost drowned out by the screaming of the ravens above, his meaning was still evident.

"Nothing, huh? This nothing is going to squeeze the life out of her here … and up there, she'll breathe her last." His hands shifted to wrap around her neck, just as she struck out again, aiming for his single eye with her nails, stabbing, clawing.

He screamed, losing his grip. Lashing out with one fist, he knocked Sky down. Blinking back a wave of dizziness, she scrambled away, pushing herself in the opposite direction in an awkward crab walk until her back pressed against the trunk of a large tree. Her gaze darted, looking for that branch, swallowing a whimper when she saw it next to John Patrick's foot.

"You goddamned little bitch!" He rushed toward her, eye weeping and bloody, faltering when a single raven landed on his head. He swiped at it with one arm.

It simply lifted off, avoided his movement, before landing a moment later to peck at his skull.

He swiped again. "Get off me!"

Repulsed but fascinated, Skylar watched as another raven landed on John Patrick, pecking, pulling bits of decayed flesh off his tall frame. He batted at them, but more arrived, persistent, screeching in excitement. At least a dozen large black birds clawed, picked, and consumed. Beneath the cawing, phlegmy screaming filled the air as the body beneath the onslaught twirled, bucked, and jerked.

Several minutes later, the man-thing keeled over.

Agitated by the sudden movement, a few birds took flight, but the others remained persistent in their onslaught.

Finally, one by one, the birds beat the air with their wings to lift off and become tiny specks in the sky. A stripped carcass lay where John Patrick fell.

Afraid to move, Skylar kept her eyes on that mound of bones and tendons, fearful it would rise again. She flinched when she saw movement.

A shadow rose from the pile, thin and translucent.

Teeth clenched, she pushed to her feet, grabbed the branch and swung it through what remained of her father. His darkness dissolved into a million particles, rising upward like dying embers and winked from existence.

Chapter Forty-Six

Jack gripped the bottom edge of the window, fingers cramping and burning. Tears glazed his eyes, his stomach hollowing and rising.

It looked to him like Sky was convulsing. Through the sea of medical personnel, he saw her thrashing, one clenched hand connecting with an intern's midsection. The man stepped back, hunched from the blow. Jack would have been amused if he weren't terrified.

They'd intubated her several minutes ago, but judging from rapid responses and barked orders, it hadn't helped. Then she'd started flailing. If he didn't know better, she could have been fighting as much as convulsing. He knew his imagination was just trying to put a positive spin on a darker worry.

She could die.

Unable to look any longer, he dropped his gaze, listening as his rapid breath and thudding heart drowned out his surroundings. No more shouted instructions, no persistent beeping of medical equipment, no looks of sorrow. He couldn't take it. Not again.

"Mr. Langham?"

The doctor's soft voice reached him and he clenched his jaw, ready to deck him if it meant escaping his torment for just a moment. He honed in on the 'mister' to block out the devastation that threatened to pull him down a long, barbed path. Rage flared into a wall of fire. He may not be an MD, but he'd still busted his ass to earn the right to put doctor in front of his name.

"Sir?"

When he looked up, the man took a half step back.

Jack dimly wondered what he saw. Was it murderous fury or a black hole of sorrow he feared could pull him in too?

"She's gone, isn't she?" Jack choked on the words.

To his horror and confusion, the doctor smiled, a relieved and exhausted smile. "No, Mr. Langham. She's back."

He felt his face go slack. "She's back?"

The doctor nodded. "Came back fighting like a tiger. I've never seen anything like it. But she's also in a lot of pain. We gave her something to help with that. She's groggy, but she *is* asking for you."

Jack stared at him and the man nodded again.

Without a word, he stepped past him and back into the room, legs numb and rubbery. He pulled his chair close and settled near, taking her good hand, kissing the palm and holding it against his cheek. "Sky."

She gazed at him through heavy lidded eyes and the ghost of a smile touched the corner of her mouth. "Hi. You really look like you need to get some sleep."

"Is that your way of saying I look like shit?"

Her tiny smile didn't fade. "Handsome and sexy."

Jack snorted and shook his head. "The doctor said you were asking for me. How did you know I was here?"

Sky frowned, eyes glazed but attempting to grasp at something. Her brow smoothed. "I heard you. You have such a nice voice. You were talking about some kind of rafting incident. You actually fell out?"

Smiling, Jack kissed her hand again.

"I tried to come back then, but he wouldn't let me."

"Your father?"

Her eyes dipped, but she struggled to keep them

open. "I guess we have some unusual things to discuss…"

"Later." He leaned in and kissed the corner of her mouth, allowing his lips to linger another moment. Profound love and relief swelled inside him, filling the void.

"I love you, Jack." She dozed off a few seconds later and missed his tears.

Chapter Forty-Seven

Stephen hesitated outside the hospital room. Nerves had his muscles feeling like water and his knees trembled.

He'd awakened on Jack Langham's couch moments after the ravens took flight. His phone rang ten minutes later, while he still reeled from the dream world and all that had come to pass.

Skylar was awake. She'd been moved to a regular room this morning.

Not wanting to bother Molly Achen, he'd taken a cab to a local motel to check in and grab a shower and a few hours of sleep before getting back to the hospital. Now, he leaned against the wall, willing himself courage. John Patrick had called him a coward and some tiny part of him wondered if there was some truth to it. He'd killed the man when he'd been passed out drunk. And until recently, he'd believed his mother had been caught in the flames when she'd tried to hide his actions. He'd lived with guilt and horror for a very long time.

He ran a shaking hand through his hair, took a full breath, and stepped into the doorway.

Jack sat next to his sister, holding her hand. He couldn't hear what was being said but saw a small smile curve her lips. The smile sobered when she saw him.

The other man glanced over at him, eyes exhausted, clothing rumpled. He leaned over to kiss Sky on the cheek before rising and heading his way. "She's been asking for you. I'm just going to go grab some more crappy coffee."

"Thanks for staying with her."

Jack looked over his shoulder at Sky, his expression soft. His voice dropped below a whisper. "I love her."

"Did you tell her?"

"Not yet."

"She probably already knows, man." He shrugged at Jack's startled expression and squeezed his shoulder.

The man left the room and Stephen approached the bed, taking in his sister's pinched, pale features, the massive bruise on the left side of her face, and her sling. It was the same damned shoulder John Patrick had dislocated in his rage all those years ago. He and their mother had popped it back in, but she'd had problems with it ever since. "*Halito*, dork."

She stared at him for too long and his heart hammered.

"He was telling the truth, wasn't he, Steve?" Her voice was hoarse and, according to Jack, she'd awoken fighting, almost like she'd been stuck underwater. The hospital staff used the word 'agitated.' It wasn't how people woke from a coma. It was usually a gradual process.

He lowered himself into the same chair Jack had vacated but couldn't speak. He nodded instead. Just beyond her bed, a crystal autumn day paraded against the glass. A few trees had begun the shift to orange and red, but true to central Texas, there weren't a whole lot of them.

Her eyes slid shut and after a few moments, he thought she'd gone to sleep. Tears burned his eyes and he pinched the bridge of his nose. He tried to decide what he should do, but found he couldn't move.

"That's a long time to hold something like that in." Sky spoke without opening her eyes and his gaze flew to her face.

"I didn't know what else to do at the time. As far as I could see, he was killing you and probably would have succeeded if I hadn't threatened him. All I could think of was what might happen next time, because there was always a next time. What if I wasn't there to stop him?"

She opened her eyes. They were John Patrick's color but not his eyes. They had never been his eyes. Sky reached over with her good hand and slid it into his. "I remember what happened. Most of it, at least. I saw your face before I passed out. You looked old for your age. A twelve-year-old boy should never look like that, and the fact remains, you were a child, a child trying to defend his mother and younger sister from a ... monster. And he *was* a monster, Stephen, there's no other word for him."

He looked down at her hand, still small compared to his. He remembered holding her hand when they'd walked to the bus stop that night. They'd gone to the main terminal and he'd paid for two tickets to Oklahoma. At the time, as naïve as he was, he'd really thought their mother would catch up with them. He'd told the ticket seller that. In retrospect, it was amazing someone hadn't called CPS on them, but people don't often want to get involved.

"He was." Stephen looked up to meet her eyes. "Sky, there's something else."

Maybe he shouldn't tell her, at least not now, but he was tired of secrets. She had a right to know. "Do you remember those boxes of Mawmaw's we kept ignoring?"

She looked wary. "What about them?"

"I found some letters in one of them. Mawmaw didn't tell us the truth about what happened after we ... left ... that night." He half-expected Jack Langham to come back and interrupt, almost wanted him to. It occurred to him the man was probably giving them space. He didn't know whether to be grateful or annoyed.

Skylar's gaze remained fixed to his face. "What

more could there be, Stephen? Isn't this enough?"

She sounded tired and he regretted bringing it up. When he still didn't say anything, she squeezed his hand. It was a weak squeeze.

"You need to get some rest, Sky. We can talk about it later."

"Don't you do dare do that." Tears glazed her eyes. "What is it? What didn't she tell us?"

Familiar stubborn light slid into her stare and he sighed. "I shouldn't have brought it up. My timing could be better, but I'm just so tired of everything. The truth is, Mama didn't die in that fire."

Stubbornness transitioned into confusion. She blinked several times. "*What*?"

Stephen couldn't look at her any longer and dropped his gaze to their hands. "She's been in prison, Sky. Mawmaw told us she'd died because that's what Mama wanted. They were trying to protect us, mostly me, I guess, considering."

Sky didn't make a sound for several long moments. When she did, her voice sounded much younger. "Have … you gone to see her?"

He met her eyes, heart heavy to see tears sliding down her cheeks. "I did. I saw her a couple weeks ago. That's why I was coming down here, well, originally. I wanted to tell you everything in person and planned on heading out this morning, but the hospital called. I got here just after your boyfriend. He was pretty freaked out, especially when our old neighbor told him all the crap that happened in *his* house years ago."

"I'd imagine. I'm surprised he didn't run for it." Her words slurred.

Stephen smiled, thinking of the man's quiet truth. "That's not going to happen."

"What do you mean?"

Ignoring the question, he gently turned the conversation back. She was getting tired and a little loopy, probably from painkillers. He didn't think he had much time. "Sky, she's going to be up for parole soon."

"When?"

"A couple months. I'm going to take her home."

Her eyes drooped. "What's she like, Steve?"

"She's … lovely. Beautiful, gentle, and deserving of a better shot at life than what she's had."

Sky didn't respond, breath quiet and soft in natural sleep.

Chapter Forty-Eight

Sky stared at Jack's home, dark glasses on to ward off the afternoon glare. Winter had arrived, bringing somewhat cooler temperatures, but the sun still shone too bright.

He'd offered to pick her up and go to dinner, but she'd declined, wanting, *needing,* to come by the house. She had to see for herself, *feel* for herself that John Patrick was really gone. According to Jack, Molly had brought Mr. Chuckles over and the dog had been more than happy to come inside, sniff the furniture, and beg in the kitchen. On her own accord, Avery had chosen to go inside then. She didn't see or smell anything.

So, instead of eating out, Rosa had wanted to make them dinner.

Nibbling on her lower lip, she still hesitated. She'd clashed with the otherworldly close to two months ago. In the meantime, she'd healed, even teaching classes with a sling because she was determined to move forward. It had been awkward, but she'd managed. Her students had been awesome, as were her colleagues and boss. And Jack. He'd been her rock. He'd filled her fridge and freezer with food before she'd been released from the hospital, had driven her everywhere she needed to go when she wasn't able to do it herself, and had spent the night where he'd just held her while she slept. She'd awaken in his arms, warm and loved. *Loved.* He'd told her one evening when he thought she was asleep.

Sky shut the door of her SUV and approached the front porch of the adorable little craftsman she'd once loathed. Before she reached that first stair, the door pulled open and Avery darted out. The little girl grabbed her in a bear hug, which she happily returned.

Jack appeared a second later. "Careful, kiddo. Don't break the guest."

"She's fine." Sky kissed Avery on top of the head. She must have switched up her shampoo. She smelled like bubble gum now.

Jack stood on the top step, handsome in cargo pants and a short-sleeved button up. "Are you ready?"

"Yeah. I think so." Why was she trembling?

He stepped forward, holding out a hand, which she grasped without hesitation. He leaned in to kiss her while Avery giggled.

They climbed up to the front patio and walked over the threshold together.

No bone deep chill. No sense of foreboding. No fear.

The house was pleasantly warm with the aroma of something savory and flavorful lacing the air. Avery had been watching a kids' movie and she flopped back on the sofa in front of it, singing along as the main character contemplated adventure beyond her island. Everything appeared so *normal.*

Tension she'd been holding onto drained away and Jack curled his arm around her waist, pulling her close. "You okay?"

"I think so. I think he's really gone." She lowered her voice, not wanting to upset Avery. The kid had been through enough.

Rosa popped out of the kitchen to give Sky a quick hug, retreating a moment later to check on the bread machine. Her daughter had suffered a few broken ribs and a punctured lung from her accident but had gone on the mend without any complications. Rosa had stayed in Waco for a few weeks to look after her and her family, but she was happy to be home and taking care of her other 'family.'

Jack and Sky slipped out the back door, sitting on the cushioned bench positioned under the overhang.

"So, when do you plan on heading out?"

She pulled up her legs and curved into him. "Monday. Steve and I will drive down together the next day to pick her up and bring her home."

"You must be nervous." He kissed the side of her head and she closed her eyes for a moment, enjoying the closeness.

"I am. I'm not sure how I should act or feel. It kind of stung to find she didn't want to see me, at least, not yet, but Stephen smoothed it over. I suppose, if I were her, I wouldn't want my children to see me in that situation either. It was probably hard enough seeing my brother." So much had happened. Old wounds had been ripped open and poison had poured out. Now, they'd all be able to heal properly. That was the theory, at least.

"I'm sure." He kissed her cheek and she turned to meet his lips for their next pass. They connected sweetly for several moments before he leaned his forehead to hers. "I'll miss you."

"I'll be back before the next semester begins."

"I know and I know that you need to do this. Your mother deserves to have you there. Doesn't affect the fact that I'll miss you though." He kissed her forehead before meeting her eyes. "I love you, Sky. You must know that."

"I love you, too. You *must* know that." She smiled at him.

He grinned and kissed her, looked through the slider to check on his kid, and then moved in to kiss her again with a little more enthusiasm.

When they parted, she cradled his cheek in one hand. "I have a question for you."

"Maybe I'll even have an answer."

"Well, I hope so. What do you think about coming up to Durant this summer? You *and* Avery?"

"I think we could arrange that. I'm kind of honored."

"Well, would you also be honored to be a groomsman in my brother's wedding? He *finally* popped the question to his forever girlfriend, Chloe, and they're planning for June. Steve wanted me to ask for him, since he was feeling a little weird about it."

"Then I'm twice as honored. Your brother isn't as scary as you led me to believe, by the way."

"You'd never convince my 11th grade boyfriend of that. Jason *still* crosses to the other side of the street if he sees Steve coming."

"I guess I should consider myself lucky, then." He gazed into her eyes, his lips tucked into a tiny smile, face relaxed. "Actually, I'm extremely lucky. I'm in love with a beautiful woman—both inside and out—and her big brother doesn't plan on using my lungs for homemade bagpipes."

Shaking her head, she laughed and kissed him. Cradling his face for a long moment, she stared into his eyes, *needing* to repeat herself. "I love you, Jack."

"Enough to marry me?"

"Um." Her stomach flipped and her heart warmed with surprise and pleasure. She didn't have to think twice. After everything she'd experienced, her answer was certain. "Well, that's a little sudden, but yes, definitely."

Avery peeked at them through the screen door, eyes wide with joy and excitement, mouth hanging open. "*Huh*? *What* did y'all just say?"

Epilogue

Steve drove while Skylar tensed in the corner of his old truck. She kept changing radio stations and he shot her a look, opened his mouth to complain, but quickly shut it.

She was surprised by his control. Out of consideration, she stopped on a classic rock station and they listened to Roger Daltrey sing about not wanting the sun to go down.

They were almost there and Stephen had given her an overview on what to expect when they arrived. He surmised there wouldn't be quite as many hoops but couldn't be sure. Nita Ashbrook *had* been granted parole, and of course, her release was conditional. Sky had already sent her a "dress-out" package almost a month ago. Unsure of the sizing, she'd just presumed her mother would be a similar size to hers, except with a slightly shorter inseam. Steve had mentioned she was a little taller than their mother.

When her phone pinged, she pulled it out, hands shaking.

Jack: **I love you. Your mother is fortunate to have you. So am I.**

Skylar smiled, blinking back the sting of tears.

"Sweet nothings from the boyfriend?" Steve glanced over at her and smirked.

"No, just sweet nothings from the fiancée."

His mouth dropped, closed, dropped, and closed, loosely resembling a landed fish. "Wow. Congratulations. You have a ring?"

"Thanks and of course. You just never notice anything." She wriggled her finger, the diamond flashing and shimmering in the light.

"Oh."

Steve had always been the quiet, intense one and Skylar smiled inwardly. She quickly tapped out a response to Jack before glancing up, her heart stuttering when she saw the signage announcing the prison off the next exit.

"Oh my God." Her voice lost all power and she swallowed.

"It'll be okay, Sky."

At the perimeter, they climbed from the truck and the guards searched the vehicle, before giving them directions to where parolees could be picked up.

Steve guided the truck to an entrance on the other side of the first building and parked as close as he could to the double doors. It wasn't even eight thirty in the morning, but according to officials, parolees were released at nine, sometimes later. It was better to arrive early.

Now they waited.

At 9:22 AM, the doors opened and a short, red-headed woman stepped out. She blinked at the sun and the parking lot, looking lost, until three people rushed toward her from a car parked in the next aisle.

At 9:37 AM, a tall, slender black woman pushed through those doors. She was immediately surrounded by five crying people of differing ages.

Skylar couldn't pry her eyes from those doors and could barely take a breath. Her heart banged against her ribcage in nervous fury, her stomach churning and trying its best to make her lose the piece of toast she'd managed to eat in the wee hours.

At 9:42 AM, those doors opened again and a tiny, dark-haired woman stepped from behind them. Stephen grunted and leapt from the truck, while Skylar stared, frozen. He jogged toward her, pausing, unsure, before she stepped forward to wrap her arms around him. Hugging her back, he put an arm around her shoulders and walked her toward the truck.

Shaking, Skylar slid from the passenger's side, standing within the shade of the open door. She watched her brother walk toward her with their mother.

They stopped a few feet away and Sky studied the other woman, while Nita appeared to do the same. She stood a couple inches shorter than Sky with straight dark hair laced with silver brushing her thin shoulders She had brown eyes the same shade as Stephen's and an oval face with delicate features. All Sky's life, she'd thought she looked like her father. Superficially, with her hair and eyes, that was true, but not her face. That was all her mother. Her nose, cheekbones, forehead, and chin were all Nita Ashbrook. She felt that if she looked into a mirror twenty-five years from now, she'd see her mother looking back at her. Something caught in her throat. She couldn't speak or move, but she became aware of tears spilling down her face and a sob trying to break free.

Nita moved first, stepping forward to reach up and cradle Sky's face in her small, callused hands. She wiped Sky's tears with her thumbs, even as her own ran unhindered.

"Hello, my beautiful girl."

The End

EVERNIGHT PUBLISHING ®

www.evernightpublishing.com

Made in the USA
Coppell, TX
25 May 2020

26433490R00152